W9-BPL-094

THE BOY SHERLOCK HOLMES — HIS 2ND CASE

SHANE PEACOCK

Tundra Books

Published in Canada by Tundra Books,
75 Sherbourne Street, Toronto, Ontario M5A 2P9

Published in the United States by Tundra Books of Northern New York,
P.O. Box 1030, Plattsburgh, New York 12901

Library of Congress Control Number: 2007927388

Library and Archives Canada Cataloguing in Publication

Peacock, Shane
Death in the air : his second case / Shane Peacock.

(The boy Sherlock Holmes)
ISBN 978-0-88776-851-4

1. Holmes, Sherlock (Fictitious character) – Juvenile fiction.

I. Title. II. Series.

PS8581.E234D42 2008 JC813'.54 C2007-902739-3

We acknowledge the financial support of the Government of Canada through the Book Publishing Industry Development Program (BPIDP) and that of the Government of Ontario through the Ontario Media Development Corporation's Ontario Book Initiative. We further acknowledge the support of the Canada Council for the Arts and the Ontario Arts Council for our publishing program.

Design: Jennifer Lum

ONTARIO ARTS COUNCIL
CONSEIL DES ARTS DE L'ONTARIO

The author wishes to thank Patrick Mannix and Motco Enterpises Ltd., U.K., ref: www.motco.com, for the use of their Edward Stanford's Library Map of London and its suburbs, 1862.

This book is printed on acid-free paper that is 100% recycled, ancient-forest friendly (40% post-consumer recycled).

Printed and bound in Canada

1 2 3 4 5 6 13 12 11 10 09 08

To Andrew, Mark, and Stephen,
The Flying Peacocks,
accomplished men and brothers in every way.

ACKNOWLEDGMENTS

Once again, thanks go to the great team at Tundra Books, especially to publisher Kathy Lowinger and editor Kathryn Cole; and to Jennifer Lum, who designs these wonderful Sherlock books, and Derek Mah who draws the beautiful covers. I'd also like to thank the circus history experts who, over the years, have taught me so much about that spectacular performing art, especially the late Dr. John Turner, of Formby, England, friend and saw-dust-ring aficionado extraordinaire. And finally, thanks to my troupe at home: my wife, journalist and editor, Sophie Kneisel, an irreplaceable ally; and Johanna, Hadley, and Sam, children of all ages, whom I hope stay that way.

CONTENTS

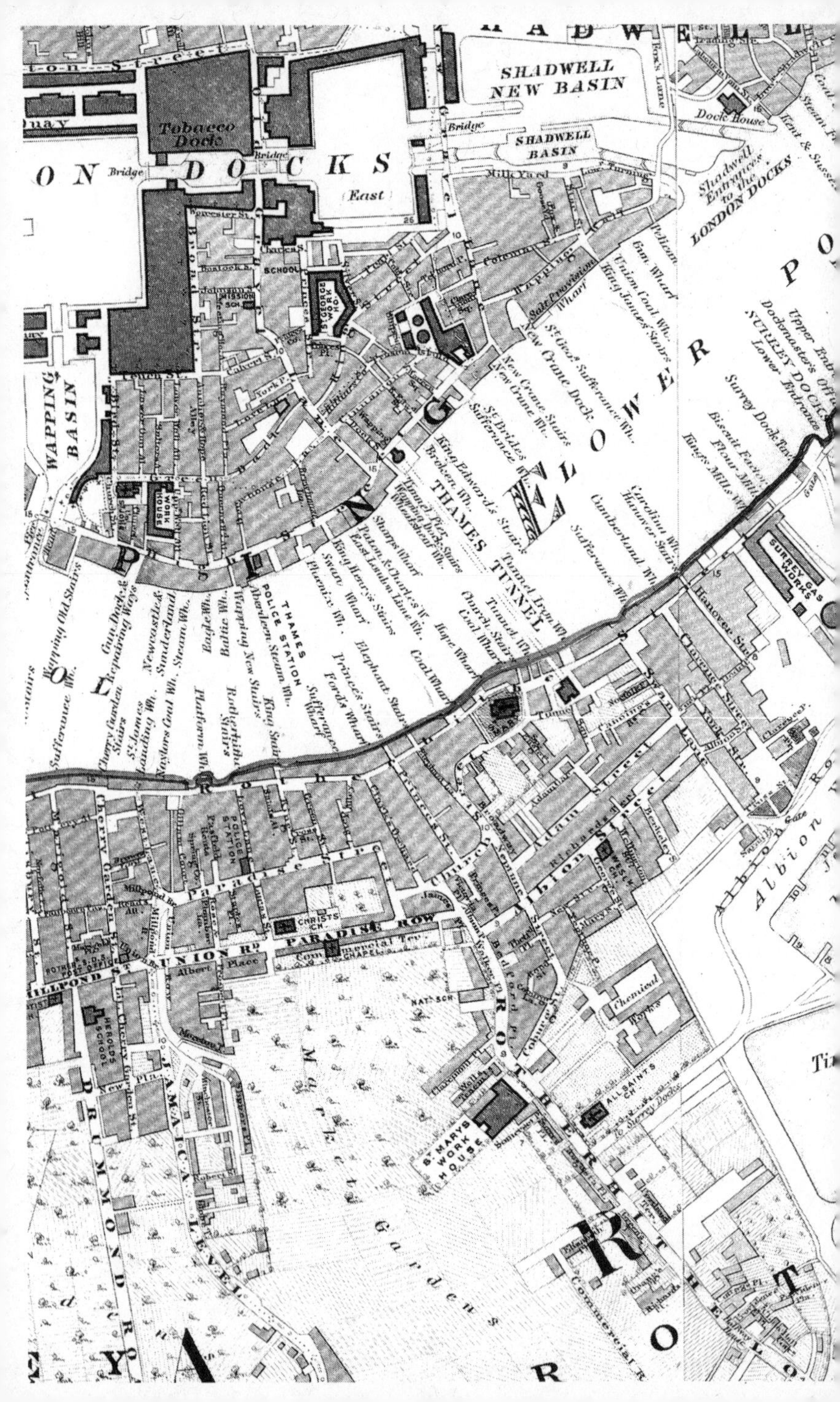

SHADWELL NEW BASIN
SHADWELL BASIN
Tobacco Dock
DOCKS
(East)
WAPPING BASIN
Dock House
Shadwell Entrances to the LONDON DOCKS
LOWER POOL
THAMES TUNNEL
THAMES POLICE STATION
SURREY GAS WORKS
ST GEORGE WORK HO.
SCHOOL
MISSION SCH.
WORK HOUSE
POLICE STATION
CHRISTS CH.
PARADISE ROW
UNION RD
MILLPOND ST
Paradise Street
Albion Street
Albion Road
Chemical Works
ALL SAINTS CH.
ST MARYS WORK HOUSE
HEROLDS SCHOOL
NAT. SCH.
Commercial Road
To Surrey Docks

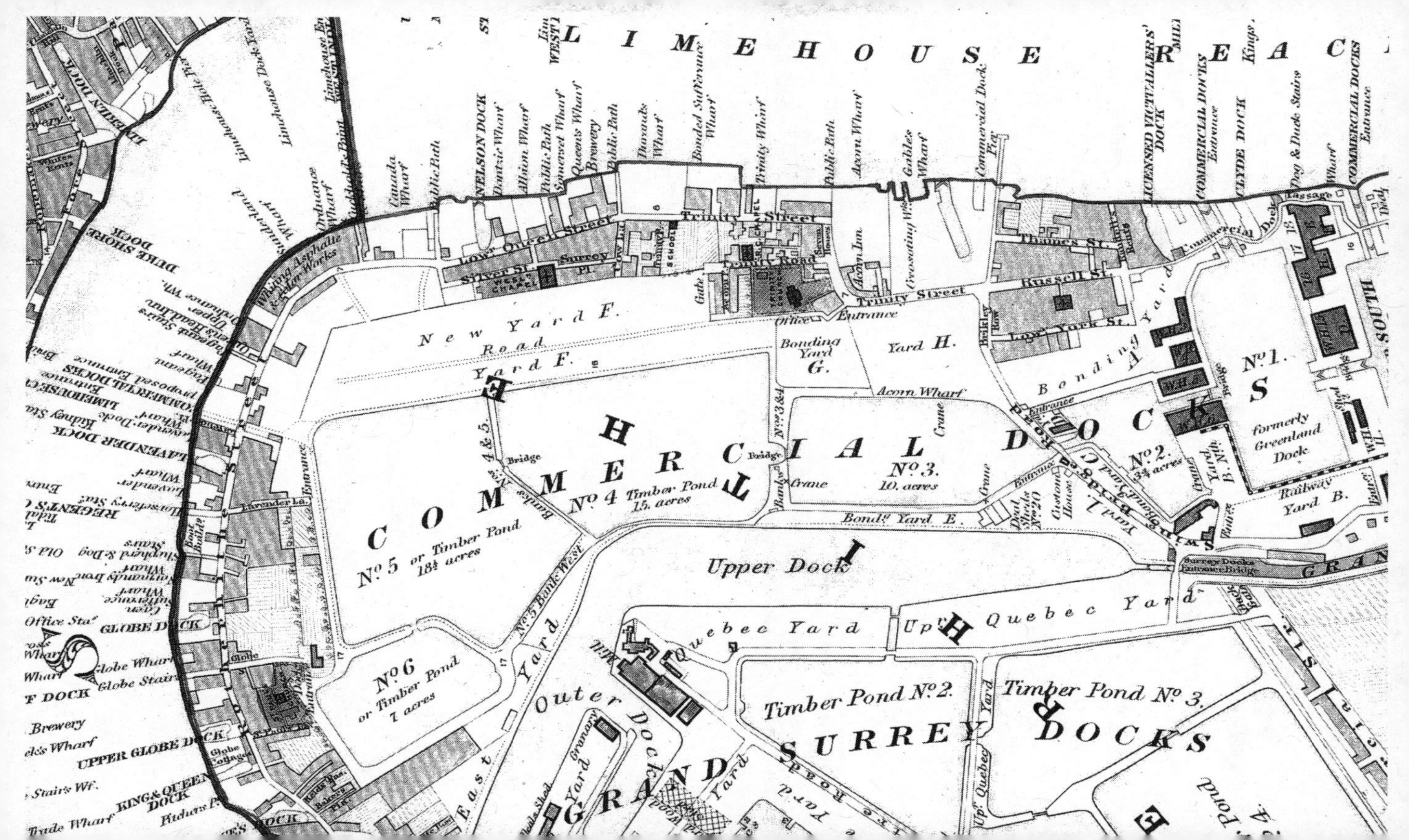

LIMEHOUSE REACH
COMMERCIAL DOCKS
SURREY DOCKS
GRAND
No 5 or Timber Pond 18¾ acres
No 4 Timber Pond 15. acres
No 3. 10. acres
No 2. 3¾ acres
No 1.
formerly Greenland Dock
No 6 or Timber Pond 7 acres
Upper Dock
Timber Pond No 2.
Timber Pond No 3.
New Yard F.
Road
Yard F.
Yard H.
Bonding Yard G.
Bonding Yard
Acorn Wharf
Bond.g Yard E.
Quebec Yard
Upr Quebec Yard
Outer Dock
East Yard
Trinity Street
Trinity Road
Low.r Queen Street
Silver St.
Surrey Pl.
Russell St.
Thames St.
Low.r York St.
Lavender La.
Canada Wharf
Public Path
NELSON DOCK
Dantzic Wharf
Albion Wharf
Somerset Wharf
Queen's Wharf
Brewery
Durand's Wharf
Bonded Sufferance Wharf
Trinity Wharf
Acorn Wharf
Gable's Wharf
Commercial Dock Pier
LICENSED VICTUALLERS' DOCK
COMMERCIAL DOCKS Entrance
CLYDE DOCK
Dog & Duck Stairs
Wharf
Creosoting Wks
Acorn Inn
Entrance
Crane
Bridge
Custom House
Deal Sheds No 20
Sunderland Wharf
Ordnance Wharf
Cuckold's Point
Limehouse Hole Pier
Limehouse Dock Yard
DUKE SHORE DOCK
LIMEKILN DOCK
Fore Street
Upper Ordnance Wh.
Pageant Stairs
Pageant Wharf
COMMERCIAL DOCKS proposed Entrance
LAVENDER DOCK
REGENT'S
GLOBE DOCK
Globe Wharf
Globe Stairs
UPPER GLOBE DOCK
KING & QUEEN DOCK
Trade Wharf
Brewery
Granary
Mill
Surrey Docks Entrance Bridge
Railway
Yard B.
SOUTH

PREFACE

Sherlock Holmes was doing something he shouldn't be doing. The police had asked spectators to stand back from the action in the amphitheater, but the boy couldn't resist getting a better view. Devilment had been in him from the day he was born. He sneaked out from the tightly packed crowd, slipping past the Bobbies, treading quietly on the planked floor. Everyone was looking up. He moved into the open space, his eyes riveted on the human beings in flight.

PART ONE

THE MERCURE INCIDENT

"So swift, silent and furtive were his movements like those of a trained bloodhound picking out a scent, that I could not but think what a terrible criminal he would have made had he turned his energy and sagacity against the law instead of exerting them in its defense."

– Dr. Watson in *The Sign of the Four*

HOLMES RISING

What is it like to see a man die right before your eyes? Sherlock Holmes is about to find out. High above, framed by the curving glass sky of the Crystal Palace, a man is plummeting toward him, screaming. The man had started out as a much smaller figure, gracefully flying through the air, moving to the sounds of a brass band, no new-fangled safety net below. But suddenly he was falling, and now he is growing huge. His mouth is open, his eyes wide, and Sherlock feels as though he can look right into him. Monsieur Mercure, the trapeze star, is about to lose his life. A one-hundred-foot fall onto the hard, wood floor of the Palace will finish him in an ugly way. It will happen in the blink of an eye; his bones will crack, his body deform. The band has stopped playing. Only the scream cuts the silence. For an instant, Sherlock wonders if Mercure will land on top of him, but the unfortunate aerialist strikes the unforgiving surface with a sickening thud, a body length away. The shrieks of women and shouts of men punctuate the air as the performer crumples and rolls up to the tall, thin boy's third-hand Wellington shoes.

A crush of Palace patrons rushes to the spot. Sherlock does something strange. He doesn't cry out or faint or even kneel to take the man's battered head in his hands. He acts in the way he has been training himself to function for the last month. This is an opportunity, almost dropped upon him from the heavens, as if he were the hero in a sensation novel. He remains calm, observing everything in an instant. Then he reaches down, picks up the trapeze bar that has landed nearby, and examines it. There is something amiss about it and he sees it in a glance. As he does, he notices the man's lips moving beneath his dashing red imperial mustache and goatee. Leaning over, the boy brings his ear up close: "*Silence . . . me*," the man gasps and then lies still, splayed in a gruesome shape in his glittering purple costume and white silk tights. Sherlock sets the bar down and stands back.

"Make way!" shouts an advancing blue-uniformed Bobbie, as he un-holsters his black truncheon, threatening to swing it. "Clear off!" He plows a line, pushing people back, trying to get to the accident victim.

"Oh my Lord!" cries a woman in a green-striped silk dress, before she swoons at the sight of blood oozing from Mercure's ears, and is nearly trampled. The flowers fall from her hair.

"He's dead!" shouts a man in a top hat. "Who is that boy?"

Sherlock's hands are shaking so badly that he puts them in his threadbare pockets. He sweeps the scene again, observing the twisted, fallen man as closely as possible, the other three circus stars staring down from their perches in horror, and the trapeze ropes dangling from the ceiling. But the crowd is quickly blocking his view. He backs away, retreating through the mass.

He is bumped and jostled, and in seconds is at the rear of the horrified swarm. He turns and walks past excited stragglers racing to the scene, their footfalls echoing in the grand performance area under the cathedral ceiling in the central transept. Before long he is at the front doors, then down the big, white-stone steps and onto the giant, fountain-filled lawn on the Palace grounds. A hot sun is still high in the sky.

He pulls those quivering, long, fingers out of his pockets, holds them against his temples, and closes his eyes. He sees the peculiar marks on the wooden trapeze bar again, and hears the man's last words. But there's something else: though Monsieur Mercure had gone as stone-cold unconscious as a corpse and the top of his skull looked broken in, this daring man, known to the world as *Le Coq*, was still breathing.

Sherlock hadn't been looking for such a scene. He had come to the Crystal Palace that day to see his father. But there had been a surprise. His friend, Irene Doyle, was there too, waiting to speak with him. It's been a month and a half since Sherlock last saw her: on the night he shoved her aside as she climbed the rickety, wooden stairs to the Holmes' little flat over the hatter's shop in grimy Southwark south of the River Thames in London. It was the day his mother died. He had just held her in his arms and observed the poison on her lips. Moments later he had raced over London Bridge and into the East End where he'd stolen a butcher's knife and flown to a Mayfair mansion to slay her killer, the man responsible for the unsolvable Whitechapel murder. Somehow, he'd held himself back from doing evil; instead, he had seized evidence of the man's guilt and given it to the police. But they, and especially Inspector Lestrade, had taken all the credit for themselves.

The last six weeks have seemed like years. Sherlock has grown much older. He stands up straight when he walks. There is little emotion on his face. His eyes are rarely cast down. He knows who he is and what he will be. His second case stands before him.

It is the first of July 1867, and this London summer is boiling hot.

In mid-May he had been a broken, weeping thirteen-year-old boy, lying in a rain-soaked alley inside a dark city rookery called The Seven Dials. When his mother had died he had momentarily convinced himself that he could go on. But then he had collapsed. For three days, he had been without food or drink, getting little sleep, immobile on hard cobblestones, smelling the overflowing sewers and the rotting offal around him.

But on the fourth day he had risen.

With her dying breath, Rose Holmes had told him

that he had much to do in life. He knew she was right. It had taken those three days to truly believe her.

There was a reason to go on living and he started at that moment. He had the brains, the street connections, and the desire to help bring justice to the world around him. If he began immediately, worked every day without pause, he might, by the time he was an adult, be rebuilt into a crime-solving machine. He would be a new sort of London detective, the scourge of every villain: not just to the one who had taken Rose's life and swung from a rope outside Newgate Prison last week, his neck snapped solely due to evidence Sherlock's own daring had produced. The boy's involvement in the Whitechapel murder had drawn his mother into the killer's lair and the evil inside the villain's heart had slain her. He would never forgive or forget.

But several times over the last month he has broken down and descended into black depressions. He misses his mother terribly and wishes he had his father back. How can he, half-breed, poverty-stricken Sherlock Holmes, aspire to the heights he harbors in his mind? Involving himself in this trapeze incident would be a mistake, just as sticking his big nose into the Whitechapel case had been. Some day he will be capable of such endeavors, but it doesn't make sense now – it is far too dangerous. He had better just tell the police what he knows, let them take the credit if they must.

And yet . . . an opportunity is before him.

He thinks of his mother again. He made her an unbreakable vow.

THE STRANGE MAN IN THE LABORATORY

Old Sigerson Bell isn't really waiting for Sherlock. At least he'd never admit it. But he's grown fond of the boy. He has given him the afternoon off and misses him terribly. He polishes his three statues of Hermes, fusses with his two gaslights, pulls his pocket watch out of his worn silk smoking jacket, and glances toward his door. It has been a month since the lad first rapped the knocker against his big, wooden entrance in the night, smelling even worse than the miasmatic London air. He was soaking wet from the pouring rain of a crashing thunderstorm and was dressed in the most tattered frock coat, waistcoat, and necktie Bell had ever seen – all arranged as neatly as the boy could manage. Had it not been so pitiable, it would have made one smile. Sherlock's gray eyes were intense below his black hair, and his hawk-like nose almost seemed to sniff the aging apothecary and his dwelling, looking for answers. In his hands was a drenched piece of paper: the old man's notice, which had fallen off the outside of the arched, shop door in the violent downpour.

It had taken Bell some time to respond to the knock, and when he arrived he didn't unbolt the door, but simply drew back its sliding peep-hole with a snap.

"Speak!" he demanded.

"It says on this notice that you are looking for an apprentice?"

Only the old man's big, bulb-tipped nose was visible through the opening. The lad's eyes were almost even with his.

"No, it does not." The peep-hole slammed shut again.

The boy kept pounding. Bell finally returned in a huff.

"If you don't clear off, I'll . . ."

"I *need* this position, sir."

The old man examined the intruder this time, noticed his teeth chattering and saw him wipe the rain from his prominent brow. His words were enunciated clearly, like someone of breeding, and there was a remarkable earnestness in his voice. And yet, he was dressed in such rags.

"If you observe closely, reading from top to bottom and left to right, as one does in the western hemisphere, you shall see that I require a 'partner/investor' foremost, then, in small print at the bottom of the page, an 'apprentice,' the position to which you refer. One is contingent upon acquiring the other. Good day."

"I shall work for free!" barked Sherlock.

The peep-hole had stopped in mid-slam.

Sigerson Trismegistus Bell smiles in recollection. He doesn't really need an apprentice. He is too aged for that. The number of patients he sees is dwindling. He mostly gives advice now to the few who will have him. He's always had what others consider crazy ideas about health anyway: that colds and influenza, typhoid and tuberculosis, do not come from bad air, but from things like microscopic bugs – germs and bacteria, carried in London's putrid river water and in the human body. He has known that for many years, but others don't believe him – even now, when men like the Frenchman Pasteur and the queen's physician, John Snow, are writing about it.

Along with his advice, Bell dispenses medicines to his patients: herbs, tonics, carbolic acid mixtures for infections, pinches of arsenic and other alloys of poisons and chemicals. But he's more than a medical man. He's a scientist, an alchemist: a wizard in search of magical solutions and gold. As he grows older, he seems to grow stranger.

He lives in the middle of foggy, dun-colored central London, on Denmark Street near where the rookeries of St. Giles and The Seven Dials meet Charing Cross Road and lead to seedy Soho. This little cobblestone artery is so narrow that its old, three-storey buildings block out the sun at street level, making it dark and frightening. There are gangs in the neighborhood and the old man must look out for himself.

He is remarkable to behold. Stooped, his body is arched like the top of a question mark; his white hair and goatee long and stringy, his violet eyes active, glasses on the tip of his always-perspiring nose, and a square red fez on his big head.

His high-pitched voice is often hoarse from talking, usually to himself. "What is wrong with enjoying a chat with an intelligent person?" he likes to ask with a twinkle.

But his smelly shop, his livelihood, is in greater disarray than it appears. His advertisement still hasn't drawn the partner he desperately requires. He knew his chances were slim when he first posted it. There'd be criminals looking to get inside his place or sons of working-class men with rough educations and dreams of medical careers, who would sneak with trepidation into his neck of London, take one glance at him and his laboratory, the human skeletons hanging about, the fresh organs in jars he'd purchased from unregulated gravediggers . . . and run.

The boy's presence is some consolation. Almost the minute he came dripping into the shop, he began to fascinate the old man: skeletal, from the streets, but possessing a brain that sparkles and a reluctant tongue that, once employed, can say marvelous things. He is a boy full of mystery, with a great sadness in his soul, but resolution in his voice, who can stay right with the apothecary, no matter the weight of the subjects he broaches. Every time Bell speaks of his scientific discoveries, Sherlock Holmes listens as if he were a tracking hound.

"Eureka!" the alchemist had screamed at the top of his lungs a few weeks ago, dropping a test tube deep into the mess of a cadaver's guts. "I have isolated a characteristic in the blood of this corpse! Do you know what this means?"

It had been a rhetorical question – Bell had forgotten that he was no longer alone in the shop.

"Yes, I do," said a fascinated voice right behind him.

Bell had started so badly that he knocked the body off the table, depositing it and various organs on the floor: the pancreas went *splat* near his boot, the gall bladder wobbled away. The boy was not only in the room, but peering over the scientist's shoulder.

"Some day we will be able to identify individuals by blood types," said Sherlock.

Bell smiles again. He recalls how just a few days after that, he had held forth on his belief that he could diagnose diseases just by looking at patients, that he could tell almost anything about others by simply observing them. The lad had sat up like a Jack Russell terrier and taken a deep interest, almost as if he were being told something that he too deeply believed.

If the boy, thinks the apothecary, *will continue to work for just room and board, and remains willing to be about the shop when I am out, and brave enough to keep the street Arabs from breaking in and stealing my chemicals, I shall keep him . . . for now.*

It is nice to have someone to make his tea, fix his dinner, and talk. He has few friends. When he was younger that hadn't mattered much.

That sad thought turns his mind toward his teetering financial situation, but he sends it flying with a wave of his hands. "Out with you!" he cries. Sigerson Bell never speaks of such evils, even to himself. He seems, to everyone, including Sherlock Holmes, a jovial man. If truth be told, good humor comes naturally to him. One might say that optimism, hand in hand with alchemy, is almost his religion.

The night Sherlock arrived, Bell removed some dusty clothes from a big wardrobe in his laboratory and fixed a cot for the lad in there. He even paid him once – two dirty shillings from the shop's near-empty iron strongbox – and became, in the face of his rapidly oncoming demise, *truly* happier than he had been in months.

The boy who has brightened his life isn't anywhere near the dwelling in Denmark Street yet. He has other things on his mind. Sherlock is walking five miles back into central London from the Crystal Palace and taking his time, thinking about what he has just observed there, amidst the screams and chaos. It seems incredible.

Monsieur Mercure will surely die. And the boy knows something that *no one* else knows. It was murder.

The smells of sweltering south London, industrial smoke and chemicals and wastes mixing with the refuse of the city's thousands of horses and its coal and gas, begin to fill his nostrils. The numbers of people have increased as he's made his way out of the country into the suburbs and now onto the busy foot pavements at the round "circus" roadway of Elephant and Castle. Red omnibuses appear on the circle, plastered with advertisements, brimming with Londoners. The streets are brown, the gentlemen's clothing black, the thick air yellow, and everything is punctuated with the color of blood: red bricks, ladies' bonnets, pillar boxes, and shop canopies. Soon the street vendors will be everywhere, their inventive cries cutting through the rumble of iron-wheeled carriages. The poor will grow in numbers too, the beggars will even beg from him. The injustices of London are about to surround him again.

"Icebox ice! At the right price!" shouts an anxious iceman, his thick cart dripping, the back of his thin, soiled coat soaked through with sweat. The city is as hot as Hades today, and growing hotter. Even the rats are keeping to the shade.

But Sherlock isn't thinking about the heat.

As he stops at a rusty public pump and waits his turn to dip his necktie in the lukewarm river water, he is seeing the evidence again, just as surely as if he were back at the Palace: a trapeze bar broken at both ends, weakened by two evident cuts in the wood. They were expertly done, calculated to cause the bar to snap when the full weight of the star was applied to it in mid-air. But the police, he is wagering, will deem this an accident. The huge crowd that gathered, bloodthirsty as always at such dangerous performances, will have stepped all over the clue, marked it, splintered it more, destroying the telltale signs . . . signs that the police were not likely looking for to begin with. Why would anyone assume that a fall from a "flying" trapeze, as this new performing art is called, was murder?

That is what makes this case so tempting. *No one* else knows.

He has little interest in telling the police. If he takes

this on, he will try to solve it himself, and then hand the Force his proof. This time, Inspector Lestrade and Scotland Yard wouldn't be able to deny him his genius. The senior detective would have to admit that the boy had solved a dramatic crime, and know in his heart that the boy had unraveled two cases in just his thirteenth year. His usefulness would be obvious, and his career hopes, his impossible dream, enhanced.

But what does he really have to go on? Nothing. There isn't anything to which he can apply his scientific method. He has a victim who, if he isn't already dead, soon will be – unable to say another word about what happened in that terrifying moment high in the air. His most significant clue, the trapeze bar, will by now have been rendered useless, and his other – the man's dying gasp – isn't remotely helpful. *Silence . . . me.* It sounds like the statement of a shocked human being realizing that his life has come to a sudden halt: *Silence!* In a harrowing split second, Mercure was simply aware that he was entering the darkness that comes when you die.

Sherlock won't tell Sigerson Bell anything, either. He won't tell anyone . . . except maybe Malefactor. The boy crime lord and his little mob, with their extraordinary knowledge of the London underworld, may be useful.

But if Sherlock throws himself into this, takes this tantalizing chance and pursues another dangerous case with another violent perpetrator behind it, he will have to use every scrap of evidence and every bit of genius available to him. And the apothecary, with his marvelous, eccentric brain, is very much a genius. There are questions the boy can pose to the old man without betraying his object.

He likes living with the crazy apothecary. In fact, he considers it a stroke of good fortune that he found him. When he first saw the notice on Bell's door, he had been looking for a place to live in central London because he couldn't go home anymore. He had been to see his traumatized father after his mother's death and their conversation hadn't gone well. Wilber could barely speak. He was dragging himself to work at the Palace and, though he wouldn't say as much, he seemed to find it difficult to forgive Sherlock for drawing his mother into a situation that had cost her life. It seemed like Wilber wanted to be left alone. And so did Sherlock. The boy was trying to remove emotions, affection, and tenderness from his personality. He had "much to do." He hoped to build a Frankenstein . . . himself.

Sigerson Bell was perfect: he didn't ask the lad questions about his past, had an inventive, encyclopedic mind, a chemical laboratory, and human skeletons and organs like exhibits for a university anatomy course. The boy could disappear into this shop and re-create himself.

"Sherlock?" shouts a young voice. Sherlock hears someone crossing the street behind him.

He is near the Mint area in Southwark, not far from his old home over the hatter's shop. He has left busy

Borough High Street and cut through the alleys away from their flat, trying to avoid his neighborhood. But just outside big ominous St. George's Workhouse, an old acquaintance has spotted him.

"'aven't seen you in ages," she says, almost out of breath, rushing up as if she were aware that he might flee. There are beads of perspiration on her forehead.

It's the hatter's granddaughter. She is about his age with black hair and eyes, and pale skin, and she's wearing a blue bonnet. She's one of the few of his peers who ever speaks to him. She never teases him about his fancy old clothes, about his Anglo-Jewish heritage, nor does she resent his form-leading school grades – achieved despite poor attendance – or the fact that he seldom says much to those who try to talk with him. In fact, she actually appears to admire him, especially his remarkable intelligence and ability to size up other human beings at a glance.

"Beatrice," he says without emotion, not looking at her, though she has stepped to within a foot of him. He wants to get moving. He straightens his coat, combs his hair into place with his fingers.

"I'm sorry about your mum, Sherlock," she offers, taking another step forward, making sure she is in front of him on the pavement.

"Much obliged," he answers softly and stops trying to move away.

"It was a mystery, 'er going all of a sudden like that."

Sherlock doesn't respond, so she changes the subject.

"There's been a fancy girl around 'ere, asking for you."

"Her name is Irene Doyle, and she won't come anymore. She knows I have new lodgings. She was just a passing acquaintance."

It hurts Sherlock to say it out loud. Irene should have been much more than that. She is the most wonderful person he has ever met, but his involvement in the Whitechapel murder case almost got her killed. It would be terribly wrong to keep bringing her into danger – he must be strong about that. These days, he tries not to think of her. He had cut short their meeting at the Crystal Palace. She had been frequenting the hall, knowing he would come one day to see his father. Sherlock told her that he had other concerns in life these days and was too busy to spend any time with her. He'd nearly lost his composure and had to look away. There had been tears in her eyes.

Sherlock steps past Beatrice and starts walking, but the industrious girl turns and keeps pace, speaking with him as they move.

"You have new dwellings? Might I ask where? Are you working?"

"Over the river, and yes, I am."

"You weren't at school much before the summer began. You know, we girls see all you boys on the way up to your classroom. Are you going back next year? There'll be entrance tests for every form, you know."

"I'm studying."

And he is. Though he only went to school a few times after his mother's death, he has used the apothecary's remarkable library and his voluminous knowledge every day. He will write the tests and do well. Those shillings Bell gave him will help pay for the first month or so of schooling, but he'll need more money soon. How he will get it, he doesn't know. Perhaps the old man will give him more. Two months ago, Sherlock would have scoffed at the idea of ever going to university, but now he vows to get there. In fact, he must. He needs to know everything he can possibly know.

"Will you have cause, with your work, I mean, to visit this parish often?" She smiles at him, but he cuts off further questions.

"I'll be over the river this summer. Not here. Good day."

And with that he runs, not giving her a chance to keep up. Before long, he is back over Southwark Bridge and entering the apothecary's shop. It is growing dark outside. He has pushed Beatrice, Irene, and even his father out of his mind.

He is thinking of the horrific fall of the trapeze star. Even as he questions whether or not he should be involved, a plan is forming in his head. *An examination of the crime scene would be an excellent start. Tomorrow. Couldn't I just take a look?* But first he should speak to Sigerson Bell: he needs to know a few preliminary things and he's certain the alchemist will have answers. Surely, there is no harm in asking.

MALEFACTOR REVISITED

Sigerson Bell has already been out to the streets and back by the time Sherlock Holmes rises the next morning. As usual, the boy is taking a long time to get himself ready. He is standing in front of the cracked mirror in the shop, making sure every thread of his tattered clothes is in place, patting down his straight black hair over and over again.

"A spot of trouble at the Palace of the People's Pleasure," announces the old man as he swings into the chemical laboratory from the front room where customers are served, tapping his finger on the front page of the *Daily Telegraph*. Sherlock's head snaps around.

The trapeze accident is in the news.

Sherlock wishes Bell took *The Illustrated News*, with its spectacular drawings of London crime and mayhem, or Sunday's big-selling scandal sheet, *The News of the World*, but he can't complain – he doesn't have to search for newspapers in dustbins anymore – there's one in the shop every day that is generously shared. The two often engage in discussions of front-page stories.

"Reading, my boy, what a sensation!" the apothecary exclaims, the sweat glistening on his upper lip. He says that almost daily. But Sherlock doesn't mind. He wholeheartedly agrees.

Though Bell has his charge on a tight work schedule, he always gives him time to read. A massive library towers over the lab, rising in several dozen great teetering stacks, forming a wall inside the walls, placed in order by a particularly complicated decimal system that even Sherlock has yet to master. Each stack is like the Leaning Tower of Pisa in Italy, threatening to fall over at any moment, though none ever has. Not a day goes by without the old man pressing a new book upon his apprentice.

Sherlock eyes the newspaper greedily as Bell tucks it under his arm and then examines a particularly precarious pile of books. Approaching it stealthily, he reaches out, secures a thin volume and plucks it. They both wait breathlessly for the column to crash to the floor, but miraculously, it holds on.

"I am thinking that I shall teach you to read French. I am sure you have some rudimentary knowledge, but the best way is to just plunge right in. Here's a book you shall like."

Although Sherlock extends his hand to take the book, he keeps his eyes on the paper, tilting his head to see if he can read the headline, crunched in Bell's armpit.

"ALARMING ACCIDENT AT THE" is all he can see.

"Thank you, sir." He glances at the book. *Voyage au Centre de la Terre.*

"A thrilling piece of adventure literature by a Frenchman named Jules Verne."

"Yes, sir."

"Later, I shall teach you to read *The Divine Comedy* in Italian. *La Divina Comedia.* You get to descend into hell in that one."

"Uh, sir?"

"Yes, Master Holmes?"

"Shall you be reading the paper first?"

Bell glances down at the *Daily Telegraph*. "Should we not break our fast before turning to the news?" He tilts the arm of one of his hanging skeletons upward and sets the newspaper in its hand.

Sherlock tries to rush the meal preparation along. As he wipes the tall, wooden lab table, which is used as often for digging into corpses and mixing chemicals as eating food. In fact, he sees traces of blood and poison as he cleans it this morning. He moves about, looking toward the skeleton, trying to read the whole headline. Finally, he makes it come fully into view.

"ALARMING ACCIDENT AT THE CRYSTAL PALACE"

Bell is bending over a pan, cooking sausages, and tending to the tea he is boiling in a flask, both on tripods over Bunsen lamps. Sherlock turns back to his task, racing back and forth from the counters to the table, grabbing mortars to use as bowls, and two scalpels for utensils. He sits down at the table, hoping this will speed up the process. Finally, the old man plops the meat into the bowls and pours the tea. The newspaper is still clutched in the skeleton's hand.

"Sir?"

"Yes, my boy?"

"Shall I retrieve the *Tely* . . . and read the front-page story out loud?"

Bell furrows his brow and looks suspicious.

"Shan't we eat first? What is the hurry?"

"I shall read to you as we eat. It would be my pleasure."

Sherlock has the paper in hand and is back at the table in an instant. He leans forward, sticking his eagle nose almost onto the sheet, consuming the story, but trying to read without emotion:

> "Monsieur Mercure, the bird-like leader of the Flying Mercure Family of Gaullist extraction, peers of Leotard and the Farinis, suffered a terrible fall yesterday afternoon at Sydenham. Spectators are divided as to whether the daring man made a gross miscalculation during a particularly tricky manoeuvre, or if there was some mechanical failure of his equipment. In any event, he fell 100 feet and struck the hard wooden floor of the Palace in a stomach-turning manner. He has many broken bones, the exact nature of which we shall not reveal here so as not to offend the sensibilities of our readers. He has

> also suffered a brain concussion and severely fractured skull. He was taken by carriage to St. Bartholomew's Hospital in the City and has been unconscious since his fall; he cannot speak and is not expected to live to the end of this day. The question of the acceptability of such dangerous performances is expected to once again be put before the Home Secretary for his scrutiny. That the citizens of London, the fair sex and children among them, should be subjected to such horrific scenes as this, and that which befell the wondrous Zazu last week at the Royal Holborn Amphitheatre, is the concern before us all. Police suspect no foul play."

Though the article goes on to describe Mercure's career and that of the three other members of his troupe, Sherlock reads on with only passing interest. His eyes keep flashing back to the last sentence in the first paragraph.

The police have no idea.

"Hmph!" snorts Bell when the boy is done. "If you live by the sword . . ."

They eat in silence for a moment, or at least Sherlock does. Bell consumes his food with his mouth wide open, smacking his lips and groaning with pleasure.

"Might I pose a question, sir?"

A large slice of greasy brown sausage is about to enter the apothecary's watering mouth, speared as it is upon his scalpel. He hesitates, sets his food back in his bowl and smiles. He loves these sessions.

"Pose away."

"What exactly occurs when one suffers a concussion of the brain?"

"Ah," announces Bell, thrusting his pointing finger into the air, "the flying gymnast's wound."

"Precisely," answers Sherlock trying not to seem too interested.

"The brain is like a jelly . . . imagine tomato aspic." The old man pauses and peers over his glasses at the boy. "Do you have it now?"

Red, jellied tomato aspic the size of two fists is riveted in a picture in the boy's own brain.

"Perfectly."

"Now imagine that tomato aspic inside your skull." He pauses again and leans forward, examining the boy. "Do you have it?"

"I do."

"Dispense with all those absurd ideas about phrenology that one hears these days – that the bumps on one's skull, prominent or underdeveloped, indicate one's particular kind of intelligence or lack thereof, or the ridiculous idea that the African or Oriental man has inferior intelligence due to the shape of his helmet. The skull is a mere bone of protection for the tomato aspic inside. Its bumps and curves say absolutely nothing about one's intelligence. It's that jelly that matters."

"Yes sir."

"When one receives a severe blow to the cranium, as this trifler upon the flying trapeze contraption did, the tomato aspic sloshes about inside." Bell shakes his head in an alarming manner before continuing. "Different parts of the brain govern different human powers: motor skills, memory, that sort of thing. A concussed brain is a banged-about, bruised, or even bleeding brain. It has been paralyzed, shut down. Some of its functions may be damaged."

"For good?" asks Sherlock. "The aerialist may have lost his memory, for example?"

"Perhaps, though that is the least of his worries. His tomato aspic has suffered a great deal of trauma. It's sounds to me as though he will die."

So there you have it, thinks Sherlock. *Dead men don't talk.*

The boy wants to get away. Bell is going out, as usual, to see a long list of patients, and Sherlock is supposed to guard the shop, tend to any customers who appear (though it seems, curiously, that very few ever do), and clean the lab.

But he has no intention of doing any of that. In fact, he is planning to deceive his boss. He has never disobeyed him before, not about anything. But what harm can it do? Bell's trips are usually long ones – gone all day, busy as a Canadian beaver, pursuing his thriving business. Sherlock will get out and back without the old man knowing. But first, he has one more question.

"Have you ever treated a circus performer?"

"Oh yes," says Bell. "They go in for unconventional things, you know. Hengler, the rope-walker, once came to see me himself. Inner ear infection. Helped him regain his equilibrium."

"What are they like?"

"Very independent and self-reliant, looser morals than the rest of us, thick as thieves, but jealous of one another too. I remember Hengler was quite put out that a more youthful funambulist was causing a sensation that same week. He was anxious to get back up in the air. Said the younger man was an upstart; that he'd like to knock him off his rope. Struck me that he'd do it with a crossbow if he had one!"

The old man utters a burst of explosive laughter.

Bell leaves with a cheery good-bye and moments later, Sherlock is out the door. He rushes along Denmark Street – he has much to do today. First, he wants to talk to Malefactor, and then, he will fly to the Palace to examine the crime scene. He shall be gone most of the day, but still hopes to get back and clean up the shop before the apothecary returns. It will be a risky task.

Malefactor's attitude toward Sherlock has changed since he solved the Whitechapel murder. Before, despite a strange connection between the two, he had treated Sherlock with disdain, setting his dozen little Trafalgar

Square Irregulars on him from time to time, teasing him, making references to his mongrel blood, sneering at his interest in criminals and the city's celebrities. But since Rose Holmes' death, since her son solved the murder, the young crime lord has left him alone, just watching, a look more like respect in his eyes.

Sherlock knows where to find him. The Irregulars will be gathering at a park called Lincoln's Inn Fields, getting pick-pocketing instructions for the day, discussing the fencing of their latest stolen goods.

But not long after he starts out, Sherlock sees something shocking.

It's Sigerson Bell. Though he had left the shop nearly five minutes earlier, he's still barely down Denmark Street. And he isn't walking with the characteristic spring in his step. In fact, it looks like the weight of the Empire is on his stooped shoulders. The boy slows and watches him turn west onto Rose Street, past the charity school.

Why is he so distraught?

Sherlock decides to follow him.

The old man doesn't go far. He stops at Soho Square and sits on a black iron bench, ignoring the beautiful flowers, with his eyes cast straight down. Sherlock can't understand it. He can't recall even a hint of any sort of trouble at the shop from the moment he took on the job. There doesn't appear to be a happier man on the face of the earth than Sigerson Trismegistus Bell.

Sherlock slides onto another bench not far away – there are several big trees between them. Bell doesn't move an inch. And he stays like that, as still as the square's statue, for half an hour.

"Oi, there's the old man again."

Two street urchins are walking past, likely heading into the center of the Soho district to beg or steal on its busy, spidery arteries. It is hard to distinguish where their torn shirts end and dirty trousers begin, but each wears a cap, cocked at a devilish angle.

"Seen him every day this week, ain't we?"

"Same spot, mate, same 'ead down."

"Lost in the clouds, 'e is."

"Black 'uns."

"Let's relieve 'im 'o somethin'."

A second later, the lead boy is on the hard, sun-baked ground, deposited by a swift kick from Sherlock Holmes that takes his bare feet out from under him. Sherlock glares down at him and then at his accomplice. The little boys run.

The young detective reluctantly leaves, heading for Lincoln's Inn Fields, leaving Bell sitting in the same spot, staring at the ground. The apothecary didn't even stir when the street boy was felled.

Sherlock is remembering something now, something he should have taken note of before. It had happened nearly three weeks ago. He had been cleaning the laboratory with a mop and a smelly cleaning liquid Bell had concocted from horse hooves, when a customer came into the shop. The alchemist had responded to the doorbell's tinkle in his typically breezy manner and headed to the front room.

"I shall see to this individual, Master Holmes. Carry on."

But he had instantly returned, with a forced smile on his face.

"I shall close the door. This gentleman's inquiry is of a sensitive nature. The bowel, you know, and the exit from said bowel. Arduous journeys have been taking place."

Sherlock had smiled back. But Bell had never closed that door before, not for any patient who had dropped by, sensitive rear end or not. There had been shouts in the front room, all coming from the customer. The apothecary was either speaking very softly in return, or saying nothing at all. The issue appeared to be money. Sherlock had assumed that Bell had been asking for too much for one of his wares. But now, when he considers it, he realizes that wasn't the case. When the gentlemen left, Bell immediately returned to the lab, another grin fixed on his red face. At that moment, the shop's front door had suddenly opened again and Sherlock saw the customer as clear as day. He was dressed in an expensive black evening suit, a red waistcoat tightly fitted by a Savile Row tailor over his bulging stomach. His face was covered with a big black beard, black nose hairs, and bushy eyebrows that went in an unbroken line across his brow and ascended almost to his hairline. There was a monocle stuck in his left eye and he carried a tall black top hat, white gloves, and walking stick. His voice was big and blustery.

"I shall give you two weeks, old man. Mind what I say!"

"Well," sighed Sigerson Bell, turning back to Sherlock after the door slammed. "Some customers are demanding indeed. Don't know if I can acquire the tonic he requires . . . in two weeks. Carry on, Master Holmes."

Sherlock puts two incidents together and realizes that that confrontation had nothing to do with a much-needed tonic. The very next day, he had noticed the same gentleman walking past the shop, and stopped a tradesman to ask if he knew who the man was.

"That's Lord Redhorns, that is. He owns this here whole parish."

All of it, thinks Sherlock, as he walks toward Lincoln's Inn Fields, *including the apothecary shop*. Sigerson Bell owes him rent money, likely a great deal of it, more than he has, or ever will have. In less than a week, the boy's savior will lose his dwellings and his livelihood with it. And Sherlock will be out on the streets with him.

It is a moiling Holmes who spots the Trafalgar Square Irregulars a short while later. They are gathered in front of their young chief in the shade under the trees inside the black iron fence of the big park at Lincoln's Inn Fields – a quiet place amid the deafening noise and bustle of London. Malefactor sees him at a distance and cuts his speech short, motioning for his acolytes to step aside. Sherlock immediately spots the gang's two omnipresent lieutenants: dark, talkative Grimsby and silent, blond Crew. He watches them warily. They are the nastiest of a nasty lot.

"Master Sherlock Holmes, I perceive."

The crime boss is just a little older and taller than Sherlock. As always, he is a presentation in ragged black, wearing his ever-present tailcoat, his black chimney-pot top hat, and carrying his crude stick. Sweat is glistening on his face, his coat is soaking wet.

"Malefactor," says Sherlock steadily, searching the other's eyes for lingering signs of disdain.

"To what pleasure do I owe this call? I sense another crime."

"Perhaps."

There is always a hint of competition between the two boys and Malefactor, the way a superior might, doesn't appreciate Sherlock withholding anything from him.

"You had better keep your nose out of whatever you are contemplating," he spits.

"I will tell you in time."

Malefactor wants to hit him. But his curiosity gets the better of him. His regard for the boy, which he tries to hide, has indeed grown, though he would never ask the half-Jew to be part of his organization. Holmes would be an irregular among Irregulars, incapable of the subservience demanded. The young street lord sets aside his anger. He shall know what the boy is up to soon. If he isn't told, he will find out.

But something stops their verbal duel in its tracks.

Malefactor looks beyond Sherlock, over his shoulder. His face softens; a rare occurrence.

Sherlock turns.

Irene.

She is walking toward them, after stepping out of a carriage on the street at the far end of the big park. For a few minutes she is out alone in London, not safe behavior, but something this unusual girl has been courageous enough to try several times. A few beggars immediately start following her and a couple of men leer nearby. Malefactor snaps his fingers and three dirty Irregulars are dispatched across the park to her, sending the beggars flying and the men discreetly moving away.

She comes up to the little gathering, passes Sherlock without looking at him, and stands close to Malefactor. She is wearing a red silk dress with crinoline, no shawl, and a fancy bonnet. Her golden hair shines in the hot sun and, despite the absence of a parasol, not a drop of perspiration is evident on her face. One of her shoulders is almost touching the young criminal's.

What is she doing, wonders Sherlock?

"It is a pleasure to see you," she says to Malefactor, looking happy to see him. Irene Doyle is an excellent actor.

"It is?" returns the gang leader, sounding unsure.

"Irene, I don't think you should –" begins Sherlock, but she cuts him off.

"You aren't speaking to me, remember Master Holmes?" She lifts her dark eyes and glares at him.

"I *am* speaking to you," retorts Sherlock, shifting his weight from foot to foot, thinking he should reach out and pull Irene away from the young thief. "I just don't think we should –"

"That is *fine* with me." Her voice breaks. She tugs on her sleeve, revealing several inches of her pretty wrist, apparently in order to scratch it. Malefactor stares at the enticing little stretch of soft skin.

"You two were conversing," she says. "Don't mind me."

But Malefactor can't speak, and Sherlock won't. Irene decides to take the initiative.

"I am simply here to help this gentleman change his life," she says, turning to the bigger boy by her side. "It is now a goal of mine. I am sure he will listen to me."

"I shall," says Malefactor. "Listening never hurt anyone."

Now, Sherlock wants to strike *him*.

"I have been reading about all the robberies," she continues, turning her back on Sherlock. "Seven major jobs in one month. They suspect a gang from south of the Thames, don't they?"

She has always had some interest in crime, but mostly because of her father's philanthropic ways; his desire to visit jails and help the unfortunate. But the interest she is expressing today sounds more personal.

"Yes," responds the rogue, happy to show off his knowledge of the underworld. "The perpetrators are indeed from the other side of the river. From Brixton to be exact. Four of them, taking the city by storm. They're skilled at sneaking into places and then disappearing. They are very clever and unconcerned about killing in order to make their getaways. The word is they are good with poisons. The police are offering an unprecedented reward . . . five hundred pounds."

Several Irregulars whistle.

"Yes," says Malefactor, "quite impressive."

"I must go," mutters Sherlock under his breath.

"You were saying?" smiles his opponent, regarding him, knowing that Holmes wanted information or he wouldn't have come.

Sherlock pauses. He might as well ask.

"Do you know anything about crime in the circus world?"

"Ah," grins Malefactor.

"Are there ever any *planned* accidents?"

The crime boss launches into his response, a smarmy, self-confident look on his face. "Many show-business protégés are found on the streets, especially by those impresarios operating in the realm of dangerous performances. They are looking for children with nothing to lose. We've received inquiries. But the life I offer my boys is much safer . . . and more lucrative."

Malefactor places his arms across his chest and sticks out his chin, his eyes sliding toward Irene to see if she is impressed.

"So there are ruthless sorts in that world?"

"Many."

"I must go."

"Then go," says Irene, moving closer to Malefactor, actually touching him. "You keep saying you want to go, so go. . . . I'll stay here."

"Irene . . . I –"

"Go!" she says, raising her voice.

"We shall see her home," smiles the other boy.

Sherlock turns and walks away, heading toward the Thames, but then he pauses and looks over his shoulder. He wants to call out to Irene and tell her to come with him. But he can't. Malefactor is smiling at him.

"Perhaps one day the Force shall offer five hundred pounds for your head, Sherlock Holmes," he calls.

"Or yours, Malefactor," says Sherlock. But he isn't thinking about his rival – just something that he said.

A reward. An idea comes into the boy's brain.

THE FLYING BOY

Sherlock is considering committing a crime: the crime of extortion, in which you force someone to pay you money. His victim will be Inspector Lestrade.

What if I can prove to him that this trapeze accident was murder? he asks himself as he broils through the four-mile walk from Southwark to Sydenham. *And what if I can discover who did it, and then not only withhold the evidence, but threaten to give it to the press first, unless I am handed a reward? It wouldn't be for five hundred pounds. That's only for upper-class villains. But it just might be enough to solve my problems . . . and Mr. Bell's.*

He steps up his pace.

He knows the police won't have moved any of the trapeze apparatus from the accident scene. That is routine when something like this happens. Though they suspect no foul play, they must examine the area carefully. Everything will be exactly as it was when the incident occurred, or as close to it as possible, given the stampede of spectators afterwards.

When he arrives at the Crystal Palace, he blends with the growing throngs and sneaks through the front entrance at the top of the palatial stone steps. He checks the iron clock ticking inside the doors: just past noon.

The accident took place at the far end of the central transept, where events that need great space occur. Blondin once walked the high rope here above twenty thousand spectators, carrying a child on his back. The sun sparkles through the acres of curving glass ceiling, leaving flecks of light on the planked floor. The air is humid and heavy.

On his way down the transept, Sherlock notices his father, tidying up after having released the thousands of doves of peace at noon. Wilberforce Holmes doesn't even live in the family's old flat anymore. A Palace owner heard of his wife's tragic death and offered him a room in one of his homes here in Sydenham. Wilber accepted the charity immediately. He is far from Sherlock now, both in spirit and place. He barely speaks these days, and just thinking of his son reminds him of what happened to his wife, so he tries not to. Their conversation yesterday had been stilted.

The boy stands still, watching his father for a moment, working industriously despite his sadness, his mind riveted on his job. Sherlock is thankful for that: Wilber Holmes will have peace, at least for a while. The boy still loves his brilliant father, the man with the wonderfully scientific brain – they are much alike both in appearance and mind.

Mr. Holmes seems to sense him, glances up . . . then looks away, pretending that he hasn't seen his son. Soon, he turns his back. Sherlock wilts for a moment, but he understands. It must be this way. Maybe some day, he can prove himself worthy to his father. Some time in the future everyone will know the name of Sherlock Holmes and Wilber will be proud. He can start this very minute.

Sherlock turns toward the crime scene and steels himself. The area where the trapeze artist fell has been cordoned off. A half dozen sweating Bobbies dressed in their heavy blue uniforms and black helmets, keep nosey people away.

Sherlock strolls past, pretending to be disinterested. None of the Peelers pay him the slightest attention, and yet he has a strange sensation of being watched. He looks way up at the trapeze apparatus: platforms, ropes, bars, all tied now and still. He's often imagined what it would be like to be up there, actually flying, hearing the roar of the crowds. Leotard, Blondin, the Flying Farinis, the Mercures, are all like idols to him, as heroic as Britain's warriors at the Battle of Waterloo. If his family had had the money to buy portraits of such daring stars, he would have filled a photograph album with them.

As he passes, Sherlock sees one of his heroes. He can't believe his good fortune. It's *The Swallow* or *L'Hirondelle*, Mercure's dynamic flying son. Sherlock had seen the boy gazing down from the perch yesterday, a look of horror on his face. He seems collected now, tying up ropes at the base of a pole, tightening bolts, reaching into a sack for tools as he works. He wears a pair of checked brown trousers, the sleeveless top of his performing costume, a green felt hat with a feather tipped at a jaunty angle. His face is turned away, but surprisingly, given what happened to his father less than twenty-four hours before, he is whistling a merry tune.

Holmes glances back at the Bobbies. All of them are looking away, not vigilant in the tiring humidity. Again, he has the feeling he is being observed, though when he looks up and down the nearly empty hall, he can't spot who it might be. He moves quickly toward The Swallow. Sherlock is not sure how to address this awe-inspiring performer, but he has more than just a rudimentary knowledge of the French language. In fact, his French grades, like his others, are always high – he can speak in the young artiste's native tongue.

"*Excusez-moi?*" he asks respectfully.

The boy abruptly stops whistling and turns. For an instant an expression of fear crosses his face. But it passes quickly.

"Are you addressin' me?"

Sherlock can't believe it. The Swallow has a cockney accent.

"Y-Yes," is all he can sputter.

"Well I ain't answerin'," says the trapeze star and turns back to his job. Up close he looks no more than eleven or twelve years old, but he's full of the regard for himself that starring on the flying trapeze in one of Europe's great troupes would give anyone.

"I just wanted to express my sorrow at what happened to your father," offers Sherlock.

"Weren't me father. You'd better get away, boy." The lad turns again as he speaks and gives Sherlock a hard look. "The Force won't take kindly to yer snoopin' about. 'alf a minute and they'll remove you without warm regards." He crosses his arms over his chest and his little biceps bulge.

Sherlock looks toward the Bobbies. They haven't even glanced his way yet.

"Was there anyone who didn't like your . . . Monsieur Mercure?"

The Swallow lets out a loud laugh. "*Any*one? What about *every*one?"

The performer is full of surprises. But Sherlock wants more, so he decides to play a card.

"What if I told you that I know something particular about what happened yesterday . . . something that maybe only one other person knows?"

The Swallow hesitates and for an instant his tough exterior drops. "Don't get me wrong, mate," he explains. "I'm pretty broken up concernin' this. It was a terrible accident. Don't know what you mean by 'knowin' somethin'.' You must excuse me." And with that he turns away again and won't look back.

It is just as well. A Bobbie has noticed Sherlock and is advancing on him. The officer stops when the boy steps away from the young trapeze star and saunters off.

But Sherlock wants to get another look at the fatal trapeze bar too. He spots it on a wooden chair directly behind one of the policemen, looking, as he suspected, even more splintered than when he first examined it.

How can he get past the Peelers and take another peek? He doesn't need much time, just a few seconds. Maybe he can tell what kind of cuts were made: were they sawed, straight slices, what sort of instrument was used? It won't matter if they catch him. They'll think he's a fanatic and simply throw him out. He just wants to grab it, glance at it, and go.

He'll make this rudimentary – a simple bit of misdirection. He walks up close to the policeman nearest the chair and stares up at the ceiling, looking into the distance away from where they are standing. He stares for a long while, examining the thousands of panes of glass and iron frames arching two hundred feet above.

Finally, the Bobbie looks up.

Sherlock darts behind him and grabs the bar. He can still see the cuts, though they are indeed now obscured after being splintered by the spectators' boots.

"You! Boy!"

The Peeler collars Sherlock and he drops the bar, allowing it to clatter on the chair. But just as quickly another voice echoes in the hall, and he recognizes it.

Inspector Lestrade.

"Release him!" the detective shouts. "Release him!" He has come out from behind one of the central transept's huge potted plants, near a red iron pillar beside a wall. There's someone with him.

Now Sherlock knows why he'd felt watched. Lestrade is a short, lean man, dressed in a tweed suit with waistcoat and a black bowler hat on his head. Holmes, who has no regard for him at all, thinks his face looks like a rodent's.

He wishes the detective would go away for now – it isn't yet time for his involvement. And he certainly doesn't want Lestrade trying to make amends: this man to whom Sherlock gave all the incriminating evidence concerning the Whitechapel murder and who then took every ounce of credit for himself.

"Master Sherlock Holmes?" he queries, peering into the boy's face as he approaches, as if to confirm his identity. His son, perhaps seventeen or eighteen years of age and almost a copy of him both in dress and appearance (minus the handlebar mustache), is right at his side, staring curiously at the younger lad too. It is obvious that he is apprenticing to become a police detective.

"The same," allows Sherlock.

"And why are you here?" Lestrade doesn't sound like he wants to make amends at all. He sounds stern, yet interested.

"My father works here," says the boy.

"I know that," retorts the inspector, "I don't mean here, in this building, I mean *here* on this spot . . . where this accident occurred . . . looking at *that*." He points at the trapeze bar.

"I am an enthusiast of the flying trapeze."

Young Lestrade laughs out loud. His father gives him a look, cutting him short.

"Aren't we all?" says the detective, gazing back at Sherlock with a forced smile.

"If there is nothing else, sir, I will be on my way."

He brushes past the other boy who is regarding him with something very much like admiration.

"We have our eyes on you, Master Holmes," says Lestrade loudly, picking up the trapeze bar and examining it very closely.

Then I have nothing to fear, thinks the boy.

On the surface, it might seem that Sherlock had come all the way out to the Palace and found nothing, but that isn't true. Little details are often of immense importance. Any scientist knows that. Though the bar hadn't told him much, he had learned a good deal about *Le Coq* of the Flying Mercures, the Monsieur himself. He's a man who isn't well liked, a man whose apparently fatal fall inspires little sadness in his own protégé, a man who obviously has enemies. Exactly who they are is still to be learned, though there is already one potential suspect – The Swallow, so inexplicably happy and guarded in what he has to say. Sherlock has also observed the murder scene meticulously. It has told him that he must come back in order to make the bold move he now has in mind. His heart races when he thinks of it.

But for the time being, he has another destination to get to quickly.

A few hours later he is back in the city. It is mid afternoon and he is walking briskly across the rough sett stones in the gray square at Smithfield's Market near St. Bartholomew's Hospital. Monsieur Mercure is in there somewhere, and Sherlock is determined that he will get inside and see him.

But he's too late.

Approaching an inconspicuous door, he spies Lestrade and his son exiting a central entrance some distance away. Sherlock had to walk all the way here from the Palace, while this duo obviously traveled by carriage. They turn and step directly toward him, heading south, down to busy Newgate Street to hail a hansom cab. The day has turned gray, as London days often do, and rain is drizzling in the sticky air. Sherlock steps back into a little recessed doorway and crouches down, pulling his coat up over his head, pretending to be a destitute street boy. Most gentlemen, and Lestrade considers himself one, wouldn't take notice of such an urchin.

The detective and his son are walking at a measured pace, talking.

"Well, he's still alive," says the young apprentice.

"Just. He'll never utter another word."

"What did you make of the other two?"

"They were arguing when we arrived, weren't they? What it was about I couldn't grasp – they stopped rather abruptly." Lestrade sounds frustrated.

"My perception was that they were put out when they saw us. And they didn't seem terribly sad about Mercure, did you think, Father?"

"No they didn't, and I don't like it."

They stroll past Sherlock without even glancing down.

"When you put that together with the trapeze bar –" muses the younger Lestrade.

"Yes, I know."

"How did that Holmes boy –"

"He doesn't know anything. He just happened to be looking at it. Let us be off."

With that the elder Lestrade picks up his gait and the younger follows. Sherlock peels his coat back off his face and peers around the corner of the doorway after them. As he does, young Lestrade hears him and turns. The boys' eyes meet.

Oh-oh.

"Uh, father . . ."

"What!" snaps his governor impatiently, a good five paces ahead.

"Nothing, sir." He gives Sherlock a slight smile.

"Well then increase your stride, sir, and be smart about it. We have much to do."

A few moments later Sherlock stands, but his attention is instantly arrested by the appearance of two more familiar figures leaving by the same hospital doorway the Lestrades used. It is *La Rouge-Gorge* and *L'Aigle*, known to thousands in England as The Robin and The Eagle, the beautiful young woman and muscular young man who make up the rest of the Flying Mercures troupe, elder "offspring" of the Monsieur. They walk out into the square, away from Sherlock. He leaves the doorway and follows. Their voices are raised, and the language they are speaking is certainly not French. It is English and profane.

It becomes clearer as the boy approaches. He diagnoses their accents: London working class, similar to The Swallow's, though one from Hackney, the other Bermondsey – he can tell by the individual way they drop the letter *H.* It is obvious that these two aren't related, either to each other or their young flying "brother," and their affection for their so-called father seems to have long since reached its limits.

"Why 'asn't this bloody-well finished 'im?" asks the woman, her bright red cloak, scarlet hair and makeup evident in the gray rainy street.

"It should 'ave," mutters The Eagle, pulling a fat cigar out of his mouth.

Sherlock is nearing, but it doesn't seem to matter. The two performers are engrossed in their conversation.

"I don't like those detectives nosin' around," says The Robin.

"Yeah, well, they is, so quit your complainin' and act 'eartbroke for once."

"'eartbroke? 'ow about you, Jimmy? You're supposed to be 'is son!"

"Maybe you care more for 'im than you're sayin'," says The Eagle gruffly, walking faster and moving away from her, briskly buttoning up his greatcoat.

"Leave off!" she shouts and rushes after him.

"Maybe you liked being with 'im all this time," he spits, turning on her with a flushed face. The tips of his brown mustache are as sharp as needles.

"I done it for *us*!" she screams, throwing a slap at him.

He catches her blow in a big, powerful hand. "Well, being with another is an odd way of showin' yer affections!"

The Robin notices a tall boy in a tattered frock coat passing by. She lowers her voice to a heated whisper.

"If I'd a rejected 'im, e'd a dismissed me, and you with me too! You find another job like the Mercures, Jimmy. Find another one!"

The Eagle pauses, then smiles and pops his cigar between his lips again.

"Well, we've got one now don't we, Mabel. *We're* the Mercures!"

"That we is," she coos and kisses him long and hard. Then she loops her arm under his, and they prance out of the square almost as if to celebrate, giggling as they go.

Sherlock is well past them now. If he turns and follows, it will be obvious that he is listening. He has enough information: The Robin was having an affair – one forced upon her – with Le Coq. And The Eagle didn't like it. Both young people had much to gain from their master's death.

The chimes at St. Paul's Cathedral ring out and echo through the narrow, old streets.

The apothecary! He'll be on his way home. Sherlock sets off at a run.

5

THE KINGS OF THE ALHAMBRA

As Sherlock steams along Denmark Street, dodging costermongers and barefoot children, the sweat pouring down his face like a waterfall, he spots Sigerson Bell coming his way. But the old man is moving so slowly that the boy reaches the shop well before him. The door is unlocked – he hasn't been given a key. Everything has been left unguarded. He breathes a sigh of relief as he sees that nothing has been disturbed in the reception room. In the lab, he takes the mortars from the table, gives the surface a quick wipe with his hands, and sets flasks, retorts, and test tubes in place. As he works, he thinks about what he has learned today. He no longer questions whether or not he should be involved. He and Bell need the money. He *must* find the villain. He needs to know more about the three surviving Mercures and their motives. Yet, he can't confront them.

"My boy?" calls out Bell, sounding as cheery as a morning lark. He walks through the front room and then appears in the laboratory, a veritable picture of the happiest man on earth.

"How was your day, sir?"

"Is it *that* hot in here?"

Sherlock wipes his brow with the back of his hand. "Just hard at work, sir."

The alchemist looks his apprentice up and down. "I had a fine day, Master Holmes. Four patients; the usual complaints. They are now as fit as fiddles. I would not be surprised, though they are all elderly ladies, to hear that they have taken to the stage and are performing as a troupe, this very evening, upon the flying trapeze at the Royal Alhambra Palace."

That's it, thinks Sherlock. *The Alhambra!*

"I am wondering, sir, if you don't need me, if I might go out for a stroll this evening? I believe I need the air . . . having been inside all day?"

"A stroll, Master Holmes? I had planned to teach you some pugilism." Bell assumes a fighting stance and takes a swing at the boy, who barely ducks in time.

"Perhaps . . . tomorrow?"

"I need more facts," says Sherlock, looking into Malefactor's steely gray eyes about two hours later. It wasn't hard to find him, but it is unpleasant to see Irene in his disreputable presence again, even if she is here, as she says, to reform him. Sherlock hopes she is simply Holmes-hunting and knows that he often seeks out the young crime boss. But he isn't sure. Irene Doyle is difficult to read. Though she stands next to Malefactor again, it is Sherlock at whom she gazes.

Her presence is indeed unpleasant here, and yet, perfect. Getting what he wants out of Malefactor this evening will be much easier with her by his side.

They are in a dirty courtyard not far from Leicester Square, exactly where the young sleuth hoped the Irregulars would be. The hot sun will soon set. Dark clouds drift across the evening sky. Sherlock had waited patiently nearby for more than an hour, sure that the gang would pass through. This central London square with its mid-week crowds of people taking in attractions is one of the best places for the little criminals to do their sneaky deeds.

They had eventually appeared: a little bandit army stretched out inconspicuously through the thick Leicester Square throngs, looking for targets, Grimsby and Crew in the lead, Malefactor in the shadows.

Irene had been watching too, sitting on one of the square's park benches, brought here by cab, situated close enough to others so that it would appear she wasn't alone. Today she wears a plain, brown cotton dress – no crinoline to make the skirt billow out – a gray shawl, and dark bonnet, almost disguised as a working-class girl.

"Facts?" responds Malefactor, put out by Sherlock's demand.

"That is the only way to proceed with any investigation. It is what a scientist does. Gather facts first –"

"and then eliminate all the things that aren't possible, and find the plausible," says Irene, finishing his sentence. She has heard him say this before, in the days when they were much happier with each other.

"Precisely," he says.

"And what facts are you after now?" asks Malefactor, turning his back and sitting down on the cobblestones, pretending indifference. Sherlock's questions about planned "accidents" in the entertainment world during their previous encounter had revealed that the boy was interested in the Mercure incident. But that's all he knows.

"Intimate details about dangerous performances and their practitioners."

Malefactor is uncomfortable. "I have told you what I know of circus performers." He lowers his voice. "This is one of the very few things about which I am not encyclopedic." His eyes shift toward Irene to see her reaction.

"But *El Niño* is."

"El Niño?" says Malefactor, turning to Sherlock.

"The same; star of the Royal Alhambra stage. He must know the Mercures, and all about their world."

"Wouldn't a lesser star do?"

"I need to contact someone of the Mercures' stature. In fact, someone even more celebrated. Someone to whom I can be sure The Swallow has spoken."

"But how might *you* get so close as to actually speak with El Niño?" sneers the crime boss.

"Just get me in and I'll do the rest. Steal me a ticket. In the pit will do fine."

Malefactor pauses. A dismissive expression passes over his face, but then he remembers Irene, standing by his side. He knows Sherlock is using the situation. Can Malefactor produce what is needed, or will he be forced to admit defeat in front of Irene? A plan to first impress her, and then convert her, has been growing in Malefactor's mind. It is a long and complicated one, and there can't be any hitches along the way. But Sherlock Holmes has him for now. He has made a clever chess move. Malefactor appreciates it. In fact, he admires it.

"I shall get you in, Jew-boy," he says, smiling.

As eight o'clock approaches, Sherlock emerges into Leicester Square clothed in dazzling evening dress: a black tailcoat and trousers with silk tie, a stovepipe hat . . . and a mustache. His outfit is courtesy of the Trafalgar Square Irregulars, a prized selection from their vast store of stolen goods, taken some months before during a daring raid on a drunken gentleman, walking alone after a night on the town. They had left him staggering about on the roadway in his underclothing. The mustache is a concoction of horsehair and glue. Thank goodness the boy is tall.

Stealing the ticket was no great task for Malefactor's light-fingered lads. The boss dispatched Grimsby and Crew while Sherlock was being dressed and they returned before he was done.

It's a pass for the pit stalls: one bob and sixpence.

Sherlock makes his way onto the north-west corner of the square. Along this side are rows of big, four-storey stone buildings jammed together with canopies overhanging the wide footpaths and advertisements plastered on exteriors. Most of these places were white or at least brown when they were built, but they are now streaked with black from the coal soot in the air. The south and west sides of the square have similar-sized buildings though no two insides are the same. Leicester Square is a mix of London: a cornucopia of its delights and seamier side. There are museums showing human and animal oddities, hotels with foreign names, soup kitchens, and little exhibition halls for every kind of entertainment known to man. Tall elm trees shade the central park, which is encircled by a short black-iron fence that sprouts gas lamps on poles. They have just been kindled by the lamplighters and a moist, foggy glow sits over the square. People are here looking to be entertained: dandies with white silk scarves, and scores of women (most of a less-than-genteel sort), wearing loud dresses with necks and ankles exposed; many are in makeup, apparently unmoved by the queen's belief that it cheapens the fairer sex. There is a buzz in the air. An organ-grinder plays while his monkey dances, hawkers invite customers into their dens, and newly acquainted couples sit on the benches, conversing in soft tones.

Over everything, on the east side of the square, looms the stunning Royal Alhambra. Sherlock stares up at it as if it were the Moorish palace in Spain that it is modeled upon. He can barely believe that he is about to enter: Wilber and Rose Holmes could never have afforded it, nor would they have condoned it. It was here that Leotard had virtually invented the flying trapeze and enthralled every woman who watched his straining muscular form, where Blondin had walked the high wire after he returned from Niagara Falls, where Ethardo ascended his dangerous, winding, spiral path on a ball to the ceiling. The cream-colored stone structure ascends in six magnificent storeys, two minaret towers reaching to the sky on either side of the roof, and a regal dome at the center. Arched windows look down on customers alighting from lines of cabs and a mass of revellers entering the doors. Signs announce the attractions in big, bright letters: THE FLYING FARINIS! and FARINI AND SON IN MARVELOUS FLIGHTS! and EL NIÑO THE BULLET BOY! The Alhambra can hold nearly five thousand people.

As Sherlock hands over his round, tin ticket and passes into the lobby, he feels like he is walking on air, rather like the man who once strolled upside down on the ceiling of the Alhambra's dome. Though he enjoys the atmosphere of anticipation in this exterior room, he rushes through it, past the pack of patrons, a thin bark floating in a sea of gaudy clothes, intent on entering the infamous inner auditorium for the first time.

He is not disappointed. In fact, it nearly makes him faint.

It seems like there's a whole world under the gigantic dome: pink and red and gold, everything sparkling in the gaslight jets. Balconies rise up in three curved tiers to the hundred-foot ceiling. At the far end is a proscenium arch and stage with a shimmering black curtain, awaiting show time. Long rows of tables, with bottles of wine and champagne on white tablecloths, run along the floor toward the stage, garishly dressed people already seated there, anxious for the spectacles to begin.

Sherlock staggers to the rowdy pit near the front, finding an inconspicuous place among the many standing spectators. These people aren't dressed quite as well, and some of the men have painted women on their arms whom the boy is sure are not their wives or even fiancées.

Before long there is a roar from the crowd and a sixty-piece orchestra begins to play. Sherlock is taken aback by the power of all the instruments sounding together. He has never been so close to such a band. He listens for the violins but their sweet sounds are drowned in the swirling, up-tempo waltz that fills the mighty room and echoes in the dome.

Every night there is a parade of entertainment here and Sherlock is transfixed by this one. First, there is a famous singer named Alfred Vance who belts out hilarious songs, then beautiful dancers wearing skimpy dresses raise their legs very high to smashing drum beats and shouts from the crowd, the Fakir of Oolu suspends a lady in midair, Oscar Slater twirls six hats on sticks at once, and then comes a "ballet" unlike any Sherlock has ever heard of: no one wears elegant dresses, no one dances on their toes, and the music is far from refined. Instead, it is a cast of hundreds in a tale of perilous adventure, a loud and riveting display.

Sherlock is exhausted by it all. He feels hotter and sweatier under his evening suit than he has felt all week.

Many emotions course through him as he is carried along by the sights and sounds that fill the music hall.

But he knows that something even better is yet to come. The Farinis will close the show. They will fly directly above the heads of the audience. Sherlock can hardly wait.

When it begins, it exceeds his expectations.

The gaslights dim. A drumroll sounds. A trapeze apparatus lowers magically until it hangs halfway between the ceiling and the floor, and a long narrow net falls into place about thirty feet above the tables. Silence descends.

Suddenly, El Niño is in the air. He sails noiselessly on a single swinging trapeze in a blood-red costume. His curly blond locks flow behind him. His grace and strength are incredible as he builds momentum, almost reaching the ceiling of the dome, eliciting gasps from below. But then the drums begin again, loud and sinister this time, and suddenly Signor Farini is seen across the auditorium on another trapeze.

"There he is!" someone cries.

Farini's black goatee and mustache contrast perfectly with his scarlet costume, the big muscles in his legs bulge in his silk leotards, his bare arms are thick and sinewy. Sherlock tries to shout but the sound catches in his throat. He has seen this famous man once before on Fleet Street near London Bridge, strutting along with his protégé like a dark-eyed stallion, confidence exuding from him. Sherlock had been entranced. Now . . . here is *The Great Farini* in the air above him! This is the athlete who challenged Blondin on a high rope above Niagara Falls, perhaps the most fearless, inventive acrobat on earth, and the creator of El Niño, the boy who can fly.

Farini swings toward the ceiling too, and because of his size and power, it seems as though he will sail from his trapeze and ascend through the roof. The orchestra is playing "The Farini Waltz" and El Niño and his mentor are synchronizing their movements. But then the master makes a sudden move into a sitting position and . . . his bar breaks! He starts to fall and Sherlock's cry is smothered by the screams of many others. But Farini isn't really falling – the bar hasn't broken. He is executing a sudden drop of a few feet, and grabs the bar with the backs of his knees to hang upside down. Then he starts swinging, his eyes cast across the auditorium toward El Niño. There, the "Bullet Boy" makes a mighty swing and crosses to a trapeze bar directly over the center of the hall, catching it with one hand and winking at the audience. Then he takes another swing, two, three . . . and lets go!

He flies like a falcon, somersaults . . . and catches his father's hands. Farini gives him three swings and flings him into the air again, back toward his own bar, which he catches. Once more they try the trick, but this time with two somersaults, and finally . . . three.

Sherlock is ecstatic. He watches in wonder as the Farinis perform more extraordinary feats, in a stunning display of strength and speed: El Niño taps on a drum with both hands, holding on to the trapeze by the nape of his neck while he plays; Signor Farini lies down between two bars and projects the boy straight into the air with his remarkable stomach muscles.

But nothing they do prepares the spectators for what follows.

A single drum sounds in the Alhambra as El Niño moves across the auditorium to the bar hanging at the farthest end of the dome. Then he turns, swings until he has frightening momentum, as though he were the stone in a giant sling shot, and lets go. . . . Out he flies, fifty feet above the tables, his speed almost unbelievable – a boy-arrow shot across the sky. His father hangs by his legs at the other side of the hall, waiting.

This time he seems too far away. How can the boy wonder possibly reach Signor Farini? He would have to have wings. Sherlock steps forward in the pit to extend his arms upward. He can't bear another accident, not this time, *not El Niño*!

The ominous drumbeats increase in intensity.

The boy rockets across the hall, passing one hanging trapeze bar, another, and another. As he approaches his father, there is no doubt that they have miscalculated. A terrible thought crosses Sherlock's mind: perhaps this horrific accident has been planned too. Farini has a dark reputation: it is said he will do anything to create a sensation. The hint of a nefarious smile is spreading across the big acrobat's face.

El Niño has missed him. Missed by two feet. And the net won't catch him!

"He'll die!" calls a frightened voice from the galleries.

Then something miraculous happens. Farini drops like an anchor, letting go of the trapeze bar and catching it again with his toes, hanging fully stretched out, his big arms extended two feet lower . . . and seizes El Niño's outstretched hands!

The orchestra bursts into "The Farini Waltz" again. The crowd rises to its feet and explodes. Sherlock cheers as loudly as anyone. He shouts even louder as the Farinis drop from their bars and fall, frightening the audience again, but landing lightly in the net.

"Bravo!"

"Well done!"

They bow and salute the crowd and Sherlock dearly wishes that he were El Niño. Applause and praise are assurances he desperately wants, almost needs. He worries that this is a weakness, but he has always yearned to be not only accepted, but adored. He wishes his life had not been what it has been so far – that his mother and father had not been ostracized because of their mixed marriage. He wishes his mother's life had not fallen apart – that she had not died – because of him.

He feels a tear sneak from his eye onto his cheek and violently wipes it away. No emotion. No feelings. Find the villain. *Be someone!*

The Farinis leave via a wooden door near the stage and Sherlock makes for it. This is going to be difficult.

George Leybourne, London's famous "Champagne Charlie," who sometimes travels to theaters in a carriage drawn by milk-white horses, has ascended the stage dressed as a dandy. His face glows under his glittering gold top hat. The band is striking up again and he sings one of his most famous ditties, a fitting end to the evening.

He'd fly through the air with the greatest of ease
That daring young man on the flying trapeze!

Normally, Sherlock would be thrilled to see Leybourne merely stand on a stage, but he has a job to do, and he is on it like a bloodhound. He will do anything to get backstage and speak to El Niño.

A large man stands at the stage door ushering the Farinis past, holding out a beefy arm to prevent anyone else from entering. "Much obliged, William," he hears the younger star say over his shoulder as he disappears through the exit.

Sherlock decides to make a rush for it. The door is still slightly ajar. But it isn't when he gets there. The big man almost slams him in it.

"And where is we going, sir?" he asks, bringing his face up uncomfortably close to Sherlock's, a root-vegetable stench wafting from his mouth and into the boy's nostrils.

Sherlock steps back. He needs a plan, fast. He surveys the man, examining every inch for observable clues on his face, his clothes, in his attitude.

"I'm from *The Glowworm*," says Sherlock in the deepest voice he can muster.

"Yer what?"

"*The Glowworm.* I have an appointment with El Niño and a deadline at quarter past eleven. Signor Farini won't be pleased if this isn't in my column by tomorrow. Let me pass . . . William."

"Do I know you?" the big man asks, his thick arm still across the doorway.

"Perhaps not, but I know you. My editor told me to speak with you and that you would let me pass."

"Tell me what you know of me then, sir. I'm familiar to all the regular writers."

Sherlock surveys him again, his mind racing.

"You go by the name of William here but Will at home. You would prefer the latter but your boss, Mr. Hollingshead, wants the former. You were born and raised in Lambeth and still live there. You had a spot of difficulty last night with a troublesome woman who stood just a little better than five feet tall, tried to get by here as well, and raked you on the left cheek with her right hand. I saw it from where I was standing. You have been working at this job for about ten years . . . though Lord knows, they should promote you."

William smiles.

"Come with me, sir."

He opens the stage door and ushers Sherlock in, closing it behind him and pulling a bolt across. They are on a small wooden landing. A spiral stone staircase winds down into a narrow gaslit hallway. As they descend, the boy can hear the muffled sound of Leybourne singing up above and what sounds like thunder as people stomp their feet. Then he hears the violins, soaring during an instrumental bit.

Sherlock breathes a little more easily. Close observations and a few calculated guesses had gotten him by. He knew William's accent, could see the fresh line of little scars across his left cheek, obviously done by a woman much shorter than he. The boy could also tell, by the man's manner, that he is a down-to-earth bloke who does his job well and feels he isn't appreciated.

But perhaps William does it too well. The boy hasn't counted on him actually accompanying him into the dressing room. The guard plods down the steps directly behind him, showing no signs of leaving. Sherlock frantically leafs through ideas, wondering what he can possibly say, with William right there, when he comes face to face with El Niño – something that will prevent the big man from throwing him out on his ear.

But he is so frightened that he can't think of anything, and begins to feel desperate.

William takes the lead in the hallway and thuds down it until he comes to a door with the name *Farini* on it in gold lettering. He knocks and an attractive woman opens it. Her face is painted with makeup, her dress barely covering her. There, sitting at a dressing table in front of a gaslit mirror, is the famous Bullet Boy. A second doorway leads to another room.

What people say about the young star is true: he is a stunning-looking lad. Dare Sherlock say, almost beautiful. Many have speculated that this boy might actually be a girl. His photographs are among the best sellers in London, at least as popular as images of Charles Dickens, the queen, and the new *Plastic-Skin Man* at The Egyptian Hall in Piccadilly. But Sherlock doesn't believe that El Niño could possibly be anything but a boy now. Up close, he can see that the performer is older than he is advertised to be – he looks at least twelve – and he is lithe and strong with a devilish, masculine expression on his confident face.

"Who's this?" asks the young star, not even looking at William.

"Well, Master Farini, I thought *you* might know, sir. Says he's with *The Glowworm*."

"We didn't . . ." begins the boy wonder as he turns toward the door. But he stops. A smile creeps across his face and he begins to laugh.

"Sir?" inquires the bewildered guard.

El Niño controls himself.

"Leave this, uh, man, with me, William. Thank you. I remember our appointment now."

El Niño dismisses both the stage-door man and the woman and beckons Sherlock to sit down next to him in front of a second dressing table. There is a washstand between them.

"Any lad willing to dress up as thoroughly as you

have . . ." begins El Niño, but he can't hold back another guffaw, ". . . horse-hair mustache too!" He roars with laughter. "Couldn't that fool see through it?"

"No," answers Sherlock, barely audible, his nervousness increasing as he remembers to whom he is speaking. "No one else did, sir, other than you."

"Professional expertise," says El Niño.

Sherlock is struck by the boy's evident intelligence and by his accent. He isn't Italian or Spanish as his name might indicate, or even English. He has a flat American way of talking.

"Autograph?" inquires the star, leaning over the washstand to clean the makeup and greasepaint from his face.

"No," replies Sherlock.

"No?" asks the boy, pulling his head out from the basin and finding a towel from the dressing table without looking at it.

"I need some information about your profession and, in particular, about some of the people in it."

"Thinking of joining? Not necessarily a smart choice. I am fortunate. Farini treats me well." He leans forward and whispers conspiratorially, "Though he doesn't like that to get around, if you please." He raises his voice again. "Farini has the imagination, the brains, and the concern, to make sure we *look* dangerous, keep safe, and make many coins of the golden variety."

Sherlock makes a quick decision. There is only one way to get El Niño to *really* talk to him, and that is to be honest and gamble that the boy will be intrigued by what is revealed.

"I'm investigating a murder," he says bluntly.

El Niño stops toweling and looks at the boy.

"You what?"

"A murder," answers Sherlock clearly.

El Niño pauses for an instant, then smiles. "Well, you *are* an interesting sort."

"I thought I could trust you with that. You aren't the only one who is good at observing others. I make it my business to understand people, and it seems to me that it is in my interests to be honest with you. Up to a point, that is, because I can't tell you everything I know or why I am doing this. It's my own concern and I must keep it private."

Sherlock has come to that conclusion over the past few weeks. He doesn't want others to have any details about who he is or used to be. His Jewish heritage had often been used against him. He will never allow that again. He cannot afford to give others such advantages anymore; a knowledge of whom he was and his whereabouts had helped villains to perpetrate his mother's death and Irene's accident. This need for secrecy has been reinforced by Malefactor, of all people. The crime lord had taken Sherlock aside that very day in the courtyard off Leicester Square and said quietly:

"If you want to have anything to do with the business of crime, keep your identity to yourself, Holmes. I do. Be quiet about who you are and *especially* who you were. Even when you are older, never tell anyone about the things you did as a youth. Your enemies will exploit any of your weaknesses and use the advantages they have. Have no friends . . . except perhaps one very good one."

Sherlock had wondered why the young criminal had given him such advice, until that last sentence. Malefactor expects some sort of repayment for the help he is providing.

"Sounds like a wise enough idea," muses El Niño. "Murder, hmm?" The daring boy doesn't sound convinced, but the whiff of an adventure obviously appeals to him. "What would you like to know?"

"It's about the Mercures."

El Niño raises his eyebrows and grows more interested.

"He who suffered a fall at the Palace?"

"Precisely."

"Not an accident, you feel?" The Bullet Boy eyes Sherlock closely.

"I understand that they aren't really a family?"

"No, and neither are Farini and I, though he has adopted me. Adoption isn't common, believe me. The Swallow was a lad much like me as a youth – name of Johnny Wilde. Farini found me in America; Johnny lived on the streets here. Mercure saw him steal something once and elude the Bobbies . . . like an acrobat – daring and agile. The next day he was in training . . . and being well fed. Mercure is a bad one though."

"He is?"

"The word is, he doesn't pay a fair percentage. Never educated Johnny and beats him as well: whacks him about with a cane when he doesn't perform as he should. Heard he's knocked him unconscious more than once."

There are two green-and-white sticks of striped candy sticking up in jar on El Niño's dressing table. He has noticed the other boy glancing at them.

"Like one?"

Sherlock happily accepts.

"Do you know anything else about The Swallow's past?" he asks, feeling more confident.

"He was originally from somewhere south of the city. Destitute when he was very small, he came north and got into a gang of street children. He was taken in by a Lambeth swell mobsman in a rookery over there, south of the river. Living with that old rascal prepared him for taking Mercure's beatings. That Lambeth crook was a nasty piece of work, he was. Johnny told me he saw the old scoundrel kill a man, and that he taught all his charges how to do the same."

Sherlock's eyes widen. He is getting somewhere now.

"I believe The Eagle and The Robin were romantically involved," he says. "And that Mercure took her for himself."

"That's the word, though The Eagle won't keep her honest now that Le Coq's gone, either. She isn't a very loyal sort, if you know what I mean. And Jimmy is as meek as a lamb: couldn't hurt a flea, won't put up a fight. They say he faints at the sight of blood. If you are looking for a suspect, it isn't him."

Suddenly the other door opens and there before them stands The Great Farini.

Sherlock gets to his feet, both in awe and because he fears that the master will throw him out. Farini is stripped to his undershirt, his thick shoulders and well-developed arms bare. Under his perfectly slicked-back hair, a sharp intelligence shines in his face.

"Sam, I . . ." he begins talking to El Niño, then stops. "What have we here?" he asks, turning to Sherlock Holmes, not pleased to find an unannounced intruder.

"Would you believe a reporter from *The Glowworm*?" inquires El Niño with a grin.

"That depends on whether or not they begin employment at the age of thirteen," booms Farini. He is growing angry. His accent sounds American too, but a little flatter, perhaps Canadian. At first Sherlock thought the great man was about to smile, but his expression had changed quickly. It terrifies the boy. Farini walks up to him and looms over his upturned face, fixing him with the most frightening pair of dark eyes he has ever looked into. They too, seem to have changed from good to evil in an instant. They stare right into the boy, as if Farini intends to mesmerize him.

"What is your name, boy? Your *real* name."

"Sherlock Holmes."

"Sherlock Homes?" muses The Great Farini. "That sounds like a stage name, a fictional one . . . as real as mine."

There is a long silence. The boy can feel the tension in the room. He can't think of anything to say.

"What shall we do with him?" asks Farini.

"Drop him head first from the roof of the Alhambra, no net?" offers El Niño. He doesn't seem to be on Sherlock's side anymore.

"Or . . ." smiles Farini, "compliment him on a wonderful acting job, on displaying exemplary brains, invention, and daring far above the ordinary. All things we admire." The famous man's eyes are twinkling and he extends a hand. "Well done, Master Holmes. Now, be off with you. I'm sure El Niño has provided you with whatever you need?"

He has a grip like Hercules, and Sherlock is glad when he is released and allowed to head for the door. As he does, Farini places a hand on El Niño's shoulder and Sherlock can see that it is heavy and digs into the lad's thick muscles.

"My son will tell me all about it . . . won't you . . . El Niño?"

"Of course, Farini," says the boy, and Sherlock can tell that he means it.

Back out on dim Leicester Square, Sherlock feels as if he has just escaped from a dream: either a wonderful fantasy, or a nightmare.

Whatever the case, he got exactly what he wanted. El Niño has shed more light on the murder. All three of the other Mercures had good reasons to dispatch Le Coq. But one has now risen above the others as the prime suspect. The Swallow, it seems, has an interesting past . . . he knows how to kill.

Sherlock thinks of the youngest Mercure with his back turned to him at the Crystal Palace yesterday, whistling a happy tune on the very morning after his master had been fatally and brutally sabotaged. He thinks of the lad's hardened expression and his obvious access to all the apparatus.

What *exactly* was he doing? He had a sack with him, filled with something. Was he checking the equipment? Is that his job every day? It must be, especially since the other two weren't even near the building while he cleaned up. Was *he* always the last person to look at the trapeze bars before the performers swung out high above the hard floors . . . their lives in his small but inventive hands?

Yes indeed, that lad knows how to kill.

All Sherlock needs to do now, is lay his hands on evidence of The Swallow's guilt.

TERROR AT THE PALACE

Sherlock wakes in the middle of the night. Sigerson Bell is snoring in his bed upstairs. The boy sits up in the cot, silently pushes open the long doors of the wooden wardrobe he sleeps in, and steps out into the lab, his bare feet patting the stone floor. The cramped room is cluttered with glass tubes, poisons, and skeletons, all surrounded by those teetering stacks of books. He can barely see an arm's length in front of his face, but he doesn't want to light a candle. Here at the back, there's a little water closet with a flush toilet that Bell invented (just as efficient as young Thomas Crapper's) and near it, a creaking wooden staircase that spirals up into the two small rooms on the first floor. One is a parlor that has more of the detritus of an apothecary's profession than furniture. The other is the old man's messy bedroom where, snuggled under a feather blanket, he dreams of miraculous cures, as a red woolen nightcap warms his balding head.

In less than a week Bell will be thrown into the streets, and with him will go Sherlock's home and his hopes of attending school for the autumn term. But the boy is sure he can win a reward for the solution to this flying-trapeze crime. . . . He already has a compelling suspect. No one else knows *anything*. He has to move now. He has to find out *exactly* what The Swallow did during the moments before Mercure fell, and find concrete evidence of his guilt. Sherlock must somehow get to the crime scene and back in the night, returning before Bell even rises.

As he takes a careful step, he thinks he hears a creak at the top of the stairs, as if the old man were stirring. The boy keeps still for a moment, but the noise doesn't come again. He quickly boils a spot of tea, tears off a piece of slightly hardened bread kept in a wooden box next to a monkey's brain floating in a jar of formaldehyde, slips into the front room past the display cases, and out onto little Denmark Street.

It is almost pitch-black at first, but once he is on a bigger street, the glow of the overhanging gas lamps provides a gloomy light in the hot and humid air. He crosses the now-silent market at Covent Garden, floats over Waterloo Bridge, and glides south-east, running as often as he walks, past a nearly deserted Elephant and Castle, out into the suburbs, and then the countryside. Just past Dulwich village he passes its renowned college, nestled just off the road, on the other side of a beautiful cricket grounds. Dim lights make the buildings shimmer. He stops for a moment admiring its ghostly, red gothic exteriors and its spires disappearing into the sky. It's a famous public school for elementary children, offering opportunities he is denied. He wonders what it would be like to awake within its dormitories. Some day, he vows, he will go beyond even this sort of institution, to a great university, by hook or by crook.

He scurries down Dulwich Road, runs past the toll gate, and gazes toward the Crystal Palace way up on Sydenham Hill. A few lights are left on in the night and it looks like a monstrous glass aquarium on a mountain. The last stretch up the hill winds through the trees of Gipsy Wood. His imagination fills with the thieves and goblins who, children say, inhabit this forest and run after them with arms outstretched. . . . He sprints until he comes to the back of the mighty building.

He wishes it was evening, not early morning, and that he was an ordinary boy who could scamper across the two hundred acres of beautiful grounds and play in its lakes, and especially climb up onto the life-sized statues of dinosaurs frozen in eternal slithers at the edges of the pools. But he has a job to do. He creeps by the big reservoir at the north end and over to one of the imposing brick water towers book-ending the building. The boy stares up at the column. Each tower is nearly three hundred feet high and full of thousands of tons of water, supplying the steam boilers and many fountains that shoot spray impossibly high.

His father once told him about a secret way into the Palace. Few employees know about it. In fact, Sherlock isn't even sure it exists, but he has to try to find it. If he can't, his daring plan will be lost.

An engineer who helps maintain the boilers once let the secret slip during a late-night conversation with Wilber. The man had consumed too many spirits, fallen into a chat about scientific matters, and commenced to do a little bragging.

"Around the back of the Palace, close to the north water tower, there's a low glass panel," he'd claimed, "which will tip inward if you give it a good jar at the bottom. If one of us engineers ever needed to get inside the building during an after-hours emergency, that's how we'd do it. The panel is fastened with hinges at the top and a few small nails hold it in place at the bottom on the inside. It can be knocked loose but will stay in the frame."

Sherlock moves up close to the wall near the tower. Sure enough, he spots a dozen or so small panels there, almost at ground level. He looks around. A sound – a bark – pierces the night. Sherlock stiffens. *Watch dogs*. . . . But it's distant, coming from somewhere near the village of Sydenham beyond the Gipsy Wood.

He turns back to his task and tries all the panels closest to the tower, banging his foot against the iron frames. . . . The sixth one gives when he kicks it. It swings inward.

He gets down on his belly and slides through the tight little rectangle . . . into the Crystal Palace. Its insides are barely lit – just a few small gas lamps glow in the gloom. He turns and closes the panel, anxious not to leave a trail. His plan of escape is to hide somewhere inside and mingle with the crowd of early employees who will enter through the front gates at six o'clock – many of them boys his age. Sherlock should have enough time to examine the crime scene without being disturbed, and then race home to Denmark Street.

Yesterday, he had noticed that The Swallow had a sack with him, which he dipped into while he worked on the ropes. What was in there? A saw whose teeth marks might match the cuts in the bar when closely examined? A pocket-knife with tiny splinters of wood embedded in its steel? And what was way up on the perch? Wouldn't that have been the perfect place to do the evil deed: a quick couple of slices in the bar while out of everyone's view? Were there traces of sawdust on the platform? *Remember*, he tells himself, *the police aren't even investigating, and The Swallow knows that. He has no reason to remove such specks of evidence.*

His heart pounding, Sherlock turns too abruptly. He bumps into a large potted plant and knocks it over. Reaching out, he seizes it and feels a shooting pain course through his hands. The sound of the pot falling echoes in the enormous building.

He stands still, holding what he now sees is a cactus from some exotic desert. The needles are deep in his flesh. The sound still reverberates.

Are there guards inside? There must be. Are there canines trained to attack? Sherlock gingerly sets the cactus down, waits . . . listens . . . no footsteps, no barks, and no shouts.

But then he hears something. It's a nasty, high-pitched voice.

"Stop right there!" it shouts.

Sherlock drops down and flattens himself on the planked floor. He can't see anyone, can't hear feet approaching. Panicking, he wriggles back toward the panel, but he's closed it from the inside and it won't swing open the other way.

"Stop right there!" cries the heinous voice. Then it starts repeating itself: "Stop right there! Stop right there! Stop right there!"

A sense of relief melts over him. A parrot.

Sherlock, who has been in the Palace several times with his father, remembers that here, in the northern end of the building, there are all sorts of exotic birds, parrots among them. Wilberforce Holmes, a deposed scientist with a love of ornithology, has often helped tend to these creatures.

"Stop right there!" the parrot says again. "Cracker time, you bloody boob! Cracker time!"

A foul-mouthed little thing, thinks Sherlock, grinning.

Lying there, picking the cactus needles out of his hands, trying to ignore the pain, he looks way up past the three tiers of balconies and makes out the ghostly curving iron frames of the glass ceiling. Branches and shadows of evil-looking trees peer down at him – a jungle canopy. He is on the outskirts of the Palace's tropical forest.

Despite the hour, it is as hot as a jungle in here too. He hears other birds: cockatoos and ordinary redbreasts and swallows, offering squawks and chirps in response to their talkative comrade.

There is a series of courts under this nave, each representing an epoch in the history of man. When Sherlock turns his head and looks along the hall, he sees twin pharaohs staring down at him with paired sphinxes below, the feature of the Egyptian Court. They are imposing in the gloom and their gigantic size and bulging eyes almost make the boy cry out.

He calms himself and gets to his feet. He has to make his way southward toward the central transept. That's where the crime scene is. He moves stealthily around statues, ferns, and displays, feeling as though he were traveling through history, passing the Greek Court, the Roman, and on into the Medieval. Each area is filled with the dark shapes of ancient figures.

Farther on, he encounters magnificent stuffed lions and tigers, mounted on towering stone plinths, frozen in all their ferocious glory. He thinks he hears a splash in the marine aquarium nearby and looks to his right to see the side of a massive tank: octopi, lobsters, and thousands of little sea horses live there.

He smells spices from the Far East and the lingering scents of biscuits and pâté from the Refreshment Department's dining room, but since the birds settled, he's heard very little. The indoor fountains, whirring wheels of inventions, and children's automated toys, are quiet for the night.

Sherlock floats like a ghost past the northern transept, toward the center. It occurs to him that he is good at this sort of thing, good at stealth and deceit.

But suddenly he hears something that terrifies him, a sound much worse than a nattering bird.

There are footsteps coming. *Human ones.* At first they are so quiet and distant that he isn't sure they are real, but then they echo in the cavernous glass palace and grow louder. He ducks under a wagon displaying bushels of Canadian wheat. But he is still exposed to anyone who might walk past. There are empty hempen sacks lying on the wagon, so he jumps up, seizes a couple, and hastily tucks one end of each under the bushels, making a curtain down to the floor, hiding himself from passing eyes.

He lies as still as a corpse.

The footsteps become louder. There seems to be more than one man, and at least one of them is breathing in great gulps.

Sherlock peeks out between the sacks and sees a single figure walking steadily in the center of the hall, heading north, right toward him. Where are the others? Then the boy looks down. The man has two white bull terriers on chains. They are straining against his hold, breathing loudly through their mouths, anxious to move forward. Both have torn ears, as if they've suffered injuries in battle. Sherlock can see their fangs as they gasp for air, saliva dripping onto the planked wooden floor. The dogs will smell him, for sure.

They come closer, and *closer*.

And pass by.

Sherlock breathes a sigh of relief.

But then the dogs stop. Both sniff the air and turn around, pulling their master straight toward the Canadian wheat wagon. The boy tries to draw in every scent he gives off, to arrest the beating of his heart. He clenches his hands into fists, forgetting the wounds from the cactus, and utters a little yelp before he can stop himself.

"Oi!" shouts the short, thick-set guard, his voice bouncing off the distant glass ceiling. "You lot! We ain't found naught these last twelvemonth and you get to suspectin' thirty-nine minutes before quittin'? . . . You're sniffin' the dead buffalo again! Mangy 'ounds! This way!" And with that he jerks them away, nearly snapping their wide necks with a violent tug, as he continues his slow march to the north end of the building.

Sherlock feels as though he might be sick to his stomach. But he controls himself, unclenches his sore hands, and tries to think carefully about what he has just heard. This man, apparently the only guard on duty, has thirty-nine minutes before he leaves. Every literate boy in London knows that it is just over sixteen hundred feet from one end of the Palace to the other. The guard has about five or six hundred feet to his destination at the far reaches of the building where Sherlock broke in. He'll likely pause there, perhaps take a short break, then make one more sweep of the premises. Sherlock considers the man's pace: about ten minutes to get where he is going now and have his break, ten minutes back to the central transept, ten minutes to the far, south end, and then a final ten back again to the center where he will likely end his watch. That means the guard will reach the central transept for his first pass twenty minutes from now. Sherlock will have that time to walk to the transept, make his first search of the premises, and get hidden away.

The sun will soon be rising, and a pre-dawn light is slowly creeping into the Palace. Its marvelous innards are becoming slightly clearer: lush green plants and white statues set among iron posts, pipes, and frames of red and blue. Sherlock must hurry.

He quietly gets to his feet, pats his hair into place, then checks the disappearing guard and starts moving as fast as he can toward his own destination. He tries not to make the gleaming wooden floor creak as he sneaks along, near the building's front wall, out of the sightline of his potential pursuer.

Suddenly, he sees a shadowy figure through the glass wall. It is approaching the Palace from the outside, coming right at him, about twenty feet away. The boy ducks down. The figure moves up to the wall and crouches as if trying to peer inside. Sherlock drops even lower, lying flat on the planks behind a statue. The figure pauses and rustles something on the wall. The boy hears a *splat*, then sees the figure rise and fade into the distance. A stack of something has been deposited on the floor. Getting up and tentatively nearing it, he sees a mail slot above the spot and a collection of letters and newspapers. On top is Sigerson Bell's favorite, the *Daily Telegraph*. Something on the front page stops the boy.

"SCOTLAND YARD WONDERS ABOUT THE MERCURE WONDERS," says the headline. Sherlock can't resist reading the first two sentences.

> "The Metropolitan London Police, under the direction of Inspector Lestrade, has opened an investigation into the alarming accident at the Palace on the 1st inst. Monsieur Mercure, of

trapezian constellation, still lingers near death at St. Bart's."

Sherlock remembers Lestrade catching him examining the trapeze bar. *They are already gaining on me.* He has to go, but can't stop reading.

"'We have detected some irregularities,' claimed Inspector Lestrade when contacted by the *Telegraph*. He could say nothing more, though he did admit that Mercure's famous son and daughter, the aerialists known as The Eagle and The Robin, were at Scotland Yard, White Hall, last evening for a number of hours of questioning and had been detained overnight. One need not say that this has the makings of a sensation."

At least, thinks Sherlock, *they are on the wrong track. They aren't suspecting The Swallow, for now.* He glances up the long, cluttered hall in front of him and actually starts to run.

The main transept at the middle of the people's glass cathedral rises a hundred feet higher than the other ceilings, which is why it is used for the great high-wire artistes and trapeze stars' performances. That, and because up to twenty-five thousand people can stand in its hallway and in the big amphitheater adjoining its south side and look up to see everything that happens in the air along its entire length. Sherlock is rushing forward under the stunning arched ceiling now, the yearning sun still below the horizon, but sending more light through the transparent roof by the minute. He spots the Mercures' apparatus, still tied to the towers, anchored near the west end of the hall. He surveys it as he moves. *Where is The Swallow's equipment bag?*

In seconds Sherlock is standing beneath one of the Mercures' steel-laddered towers. The police ropes have been removed, the suspicious trapeze bar taken away. But there is The Swallow's satchel, partway up the tower, maybe twenty feet high, and tied down. Sherlock looks farther up and sees that the swings belonging to the three younger troupe members have been pulled up to the perch, more than a hundred and fifty feet above the floor. He feels dizzy and reaches out to grab the tower.

He had planned to climb boldly to the perch and examine it, and not just because he might find sawdust left behind, but because it is such a marvelous, unreachable place to hide something.

But now, staring up and feeling ill, his ambition wavers. His heart is pounding and his pin-cushioned hands ache. The short distance to The Swallow's equipment seems daunting enough. But all the way up to the top? He has no idea if he can do it. If he tries, will he freeze partway up? But he can't falter, not now, not when he's so close. He is running out of time. He starts arguing with himself, making the point that he may have enough to investigate here on the floor and up there at twenty feet high, where that mysterious –

A sound comes down the central transept toward him.

Footsteps again. This time they are moving at a hurried pace. *Why has the guard arrived so quickly?*

Sherlock considers his situation for an instant. If he runs, his chances of being spotted will increase. And since it seems like the guard knows where he is, the dogs will sniff him out no matter where he goes . . . that is, if he stays on the ground.

He looks up the terrifying tower at the perch.

He has only one option.

He starts to climb.

UP IN THE AIR

It is a sort of paralyzing feeling: the one that invades your body when you are high in the air and petrified and you have no option but to go higher. It is like Sherlock has stepped up onto the tower and entered a nightmare. He'd had no idea whether or not he was afraid of heights, had never been at any extreme elevation. But now he knows.

He is.

Both Sigerson Bell and his father have spoken to him about adrenaline. It is a liquid compound of some sort that some organ in your body secretes when you are terrified, when you want to run, when you are extremely excited. Adrenaline is pouring through his body at the rate beer flows out of the taps that fill the barrels in the many breweries on the Thames. He staggers up the cast-iron tower like a drunk, his legs rubbery, his heart slamming in his chest, feeling for each rung, slipping and falling . . . and still climbing. He is gasping and making noise, completely giving away his whereabouts.

In the midst of his terror, he starts thinking that something doesn't make sense about this pursuit. And then it dawns on him. Why aren't the bull terriers barking? It is a curious fact – the dogs are not making noise in the night. He looks down and sees the man standing at the bottom of the tower where it is bolted to the floor, his head down, concentrating on putting his foot securely on the first rung.

His beasts aren't with him!

The boy is being pursued by dogs that not only make no sound, but don't exist.

And the man . . . isn't a man.

When his assailant looks up, Sherlock can see the face of The Swallow glaring at him.

So, this is his position: he is being chased up a one-hundred-and-fifty-foot cast-iron ladder by a professional trapeze artiste, as at home in the sky as a bird, a lad younger than he, but as strong as a tiger . . . a physically skilled, violent boy, trained to kill at a young age, who appears to have just murdered someone, and who will undoubtedly stop at nothing to conceal that fact. The Swallow now knows that the police think it was foul play; he knows that Sherlock was snooping around yesterday and saw him examining and tying up the trapeze bars, and that he is responsible for maintaining the troupe's safety. The young snoop is in The Swallow's sights, way up the tower in a near-deserted building . . . a perfect place to kill.

Sherlock can't believe this is happening. Why, oh why, did he decide to investigate this murder? It's turning out to be as violent as the Whitechapel case. He should have let Sigerson Bell fend for himself, and found other ways to get money for school – *steal*, for God's sake.

He looks down and then back up. He has no choice. He must keep going toward the glass ceiling. He scurries skyward like a squirrel.

But The Swallow shortens the distance between them in a flash. He climbs at twice Sherlock's speed. The tall, thin boy thinks he should calculate how long it will take L'Hirondelle to catch him, but he doesn't. It doesn't matter now. He simply has to *move*! He can't fight the young athlete here. Maybe, if he gets to the perch first, he can think of something, have some sort of advantage. *Maybe.*

He decides to not look down. Turning his face upward, he makes for the perch with all he has.

He nears it. But The Swallow seems to be picking up speed.

"Boy!" he shouts.

Then Sherlock hears dogs barking down the hall in the northern transept. *They* are coming too.

His hand reaches the perch. He can feel his pursuer's steps shaking the tower just a foot or two beneath him! He seizes the thick wooden surface and tries to swing himself up onto it. His grip slips, he loses his footing and falls, out into the space high in the Crystal Palace, toward its hard wooden floor a hundred and fifty feet below! He clutches at the perch again . . . and somehow grasps it with one hand. He tries to raise himself but can't – he doesn't have the strength. He feels The Swallow's hand grabbing for him, grazing his boot, and with a Herculean effort reaches up with his other hand, grips the platform and pulls himself up onto it. He has no idea how he found the power.

Standing up, looking out over the edge of the perch at the two tiny dogs and man far below, he almost faints. It is an incredible sight. He can't imagine how the Mercures, how El Niño, does it. For an instant, a strange, almost exhilarating feeling creeps into the pit of his stomach and makes him feel like giving up. Why doesn't he just fall into the air and float downward the way you would at the end of a wonderful dream?

The Swallow's eyes appear over the edge of the platform. Sherlock pivots and kicks at him, aiming the point of his shoe right for his nose, but the boy, his face calm and collected, reacts like lightening and seizes the foot. Sherlock stumbles and as he does one of his arms windmills in the air and knocks a trapeze bar from its hook on the tower just behind him, above his head. At the same time, he jerks his foot back and starts to fall again. He is going over the edge of the platform . . . out into space for good. *Sherlock Holmes is dead.* It's like he is falling down a waterfall, plummeting to his destiny.

But at the last split second he spots the trapeze bar above, loosed now, and also swinging out over the open space.

He snatches it with both hands.

In an instant, Sherlock is flying through the air . . . with the least of ease.

He swings out over the central transept, holding on for dear life, his black frock coat fluttering as he swoops, his injured hands screaming.

Sherlock can't breathe. He sees almost everything in

the monster building, all the way down the north hallway to the end. He spots something curious – a small room at the western side of the transept, enclosed by a wall that doesn't quite reach the ceiling. But he can't see into it and it passes through his sight in a second and rushes past. He flails about in the air. He doesn't know what to do. How do they move up here? Perhaps he can land way over on the other perch, on Monsieur Mercure's boards on the other tower? He passes the bottom of the pendulum swing and is now climbing toward Mercure's platform. He thinks of El Niño, kicking his legs as he flew to gain speed, so he tries that, but it has little effect. He tries again, amazed at the way it hurts his abdomen, and feels a slight push, upward toward the perch.

But when the platform is right beside him, he can't get his long legs onto it, doesn't have the vigor in his intestinal muscles to lift them high enough to set his feet onto the wooden surface. He misses and starts to go backward, on another gigantic swing in the direction he came from . . . toward The Swallow and the first perch. He is so terrified that he doesn't care what happens. He just wants to get off. As he climbs the air near the first perch, he does something desperate. He lets go, hoping his momentum can simply shoot him up onto the platform, maybe even knock The Swallow down.

But it doesn't.

He misses the perch altogether.

But something unexpected happens. He sticks one foot into a rung on the tower to brace himself, reaches out

8

A SWALLOW'S LIFE

Sherlock won't have to mingle with the early-arriving employees in order to get out of the building. He is under the safe wing of the young trapeze star. The Palace apparently has a room where performers can stay during engagements. The Swallow had been fast asleep when he heard someone near the apparatus. He explains to the guard, who can barely control his excited beasts, that this boy is his guest, and that though an accident had nearly occurred when they went up to the perch together for a spectacular view, everything is perfectly under control now.

The young star is lying for him.

It is evident that this boy did not make those cuts in Monsieur Mercure's trapeze bar. If he had, he wouldn't be doing this, and more to the point, he would have let Sherlock fall. *But if it wasn't The Swallow, then who?*

"Why were you up there?" the acrobat asks as they sit in the wooden seats in the nearby amphitheater.

Sherlock feels it is time to be just as honest with The Swallow as he was with El Niño. It will be to his advantage to have the boy on his side.

"I was here on the day of the accident. Mercure landed almost at my feet when he fell. I noticed two cuts in his bar."

The young detective watches The Swallow's reaction. He seems truly shocked.

"But why?" he asks. "Who would want to kill 'im?"

"You," says Sherlock, rubbing his sore hands.

"Me? 'e's a cad, but 'e's me meal ticket. I ain't a fool."

"You used to run with a Lambeth gang. Your boss taught you all sorts of skullduggery. He showed you how to kill."

The Swallow gazes at Sherlock for a moment. His dark eyes turn hard under his tousled black hair.

"You seem to know a lot about me, you do."

"I have made it my business to."

"Then what's your business and who are you?" The young athlete stands up.

"I can't tell you much about myself. But I can tell you a few things about this murder. And that's what it is. First, I know you didn't do it and I can prove it."

The comment has the desired effect. The Swallow sits down again, relieved.

"My name is Sherlock Holmes and I need you to cooperate with me."

"Much obliged to do so."

Sherlock likes this boy, not only because he has just saved his life, but because he can obviously size up situations quickly.

"Tell me more about yourself, Johnny."

Taken aback by Sherlock's use of his real name, The Swallow pauses for a few seconds before talking:

"Not much I can say either, mate," he winks. "Grew up in Brixton south o' Lambeth in the Laursten Gardens neighborhood, a kind of down-and-out place with scads o' empty houses. Me guvna were a bad 'un and run off on me mum. Nineteen of us, family and others, livin' in one flat, children across the bottom o' three straw beds, a bucket in the center o' the room for the whole lot. I got in with bad sorts and went north some steps to Lambeth, closer to the action. Thought I was a big 'un, I did. Learned 'ow to nick, 'ow to pluck pockets, and yeah, 'ow to do in a man if I needed to."

"How long has your mother been dead?"

How in the name of Leotard does he know that? wonders The Swallow. He decides this lad must be some sort of magician, just like those wits, The Davenport Brothers, who pretend they read minds on stage.

"Trained in our business, Master 'olmes?"

"No, by a scientist. Observation, Master Wilde, that's all it is. I noticed the ring on your left hand. It is obviously a woman's. You were wearing it while you slept, so you must never take it off. Had to be your mother's – you are too young to be walking out with a girl."

"She's dead more than a twelvemonth now, dear mum. I supports the little 'uns."

Sherlock was getting a clearer picture of one Jonathan Wilde, born Brixton, late of the Lambeth streets, also known as The Swallow. Tough on the outside, but a marshmallow inside, not really suited in the end to steal or kill; someone who might be persuaded to help find the real villain.

"I want you to keep your eyes open for me."

"It 'ud be me pleasure. I don't takes kindly to sliced trapeze bars."

"If you remember anything else that you should have told me, let me know."

"I shall."

Sherlock is about to leave. The sun has risen. He has to get back to London on the double. But his mind is racing too – there are so many questions to ask this boy. Sherlock hadn't, for example, been satisfied with the flippant answer The Swallow had given him yesterday about Mercure's enemies. Perhaps he'll do better now. This time, Sherlock will phrase the question carefully.

"In your opinion, is there anyone from outside the profession who might want to do away with Monsieur Mercure?"

"Not outside the business, no. But then, I don't know many people other than show folks now."

"Did he have any debts?"

"'im? 'e had a load of coins stacked as 'igh as they is in the Bank of England, 'e did. And 'e weren't sharin' it, believe me."

"Noticed any suspicious people loitering about these past few days?"

"No . . ." begins The Swallow, stopping in mid-sentence. His eyes seem to register some recollection, then jump back into the present. "No," he says, "definitely not, just the usual sort."

Sherlock notices the pause and places it in his memory. This Swallow is an interesting young man, and he may prove to be even more so in the near future.

On his way home, Sherlock rushes through Trafalgar Square, then speeds north on a wide, busy street past palatial steps that lead to the huge doors of a towering church. As he turns his head to glance at it, someone violently seizes him and pulls him into the mews across the street on the far side of St. Martin's ominous granite workhouse. Good and evil are often side by side in London.

"Master Holmes, I perceive."

"Malefactor."

The young leader is alone and smiling, his sunken eyes look sharp and mischievous. He clutches a newspaper in his hand, obviously amused at something. His slight Irish accent grows stronger when he's angry or excited. "Have you seen this?" he asks, his tongue darting out of his mouth like a reptile's. He is holding up *The Illustrated Police News* to display its headline: "MURDER AT THE PALACE?"

"I know of it," answers the boy, trying to recover his equanimity without showing he ever lost it, fixing the disturbed collar on his frock coat.

"Care for a clue?" asks Malefactor pompously.

"I have several."

Sherlock has actually been thinking precisely the opposite: that he has none. He is back at the beginning of this investigation, miles from his reward. If The Swallow didn't do it and neither did the meek Eagle, then his only suspect is The Robin and she isn't a good one. El Niño had described her as disloyal, and she didn't seem terribly impressed with her beau when Sherlock saw them talking, so it seems doubtful that she really cares for the younger man *or* the older – that she has the passion to kill Mercure, or would sacrifice anything for The Eagle. Her only loyalty is to the troupe's name and the fame and money it brings her, whether its leader is alive or dead. She has no real motive.

"I am in possession of information about the chap known to the applauding masses as . . . The Swallow," says Malefactor smugly, bowing deeply as if he were on the Alhambra stage.

There is a brief pause. Sherlock is reluctant to ask about it. But his rival will make him. The young master thief is greatly enjoying the attentions of Irene Doyle these days and having something important to tell Sherlock about this case, something the boy is anxious to know, just adds to his fun. He grins at Holmes, waiting for him to grovel, to beg to know what he knows.

What could this criminal, an expert among thieves and murderers, know about one of London's greatest young trapeze stars?

"What is it?" the boy detective finally inquires brusquely.

"He was born and spent his early days in Brixton."

Sherlock grins.

"Oh really?"

"Really," says Malefactor, examining his fingernails. "You seem unimpressed."

"Because I discovered that fact long ago." It is only partly a lie. He begins to examine his own nails, then notices and stops. He straightens his hair, notices that too, and puts his hands at his side.

"I was just getting started, Master Genius." Malefactor looks daggers at him and smoothes out his precious tailcoat. "But given your attitude, I don't think I shall go on. Suffice it to say that you should be aware of more than just the simple whereabouts of Master Swallow's early years. Rather, you should consider its significance. I shall tell you nothing more. I have said too much as it is, anyway."

"That is fine with me," snaps Sherlock. "I don't need help from the likes of you anymore. I suggest you go back to stealing."

"While *you* seek justice and do what is right for the British Empire?" growls Malefactor.

"I shall do the first part, anyway."

"You are no better than me. There is none of us any better than the other."

"I beg to differ."

"There are no such things as good and evil. There are simply human machinations: people trying to survive and thrive. I learned that long ago."

Sherlock has deduced a great deal about the other boy since he first met him last year: from things he has said, from that precious, once-luxurious tailcoat that he cleans almost daily. This boy was once in much better circumstances, perhaps in Ireland. He has suffered a great fall. Someone caused it. He has about him the mental wherewithal to be much more than he is – he's been well educated and taught social graces.

But Sherlock and his family fell too – his mother from a mighty height – and he has chosen to seek good while Malefactor hasn't. They both came to a crossroads in life and made their choices.

"I am someone whose morals you profess to abhor," hisses Malefactor. "Yet you use me to get what you want." He is seething, barely restraining himself. "And you will continue to *try* to use me as long as you get something from it! As long as it helps you become something greater than you are, makes you feel like someone special . . . the great detective!"

"I –"

"You cannot deny it!"

A middle-class couple, dressed up to look as upper-class as they can in matching blue silk dress with crinoline and navy bonnet, and black frock coat and blue waistcoat with tall top hat, are passing on St. Martin's Lane near the church beyond the mews. They stop for an instant and look down the narrow alley toward the two tall boys dressed in their worn outfits. The couple quickly moves on.

"You would use evil to make good," snarls Malefactor.

"That is nonsense." Sherlock swallows and tries not to look away from his opponent.

"But it seems . . . that I have the girl."

There is silence. Their big heads are close and, neither

blinking, they look into each other's gray eyes. When Sherlock speaks, a dab of spittle flies out of his mouth and lands on Malefactor's cheek.

"I don't need her . . . or you."

And with that he turns and stomps down the mews without looking back, heading toward his Denmark Street lodgings.

"The Swallow pretends that he is reformed! No one reforms!" shouts the young criminal after him. Then he smiles, thinking of the seed he has sewn in Holmes' mind. In an instant he is heading south to find his gang.

Sherlock holds his hands over his ears as he marches away. He is trying not to think of what Malefactor said and why he said it, or what he means by . . . He stops himself and tries to shift his mind to other things.

He runs angrily through the early morning crowds, amidst the noise of London: the roll of iron wheels and the clap of horses' hooves on stones, shouts of people wanting and needing things; that admixture of colors, of gentlemen and ladies and beggars and singing vendors. He swings away from the dangerous little streets of The Seven Dials, thinking about good and evil, imagining the desperate folks who congregate there, some bad people indeed, others simply half-clothed and needy. He thinks of the strange alloy of buildings on Endell Street on the Dials' east side: another massive workhouse for those who have fallen, side by side with a hospital. Good and bad together there too. It's that way all over London. Desperation is here in St. Giles, but just north above Oxford Street, the rich float through life. It is said that if you want to see poverty in the city, just cross the street; if you want luxury, cross back.

"Watch it, blackguard!" shouts a crazy, old toothless woman with dead flowers in her hand, which she is trying to sell. Sherlock had dodged a smelly cart pushed by a cheesemonger and nearly knocked her down.

He tries to shut off his mind and focus on getting home quickly. The corner of Crown and Denmark streets is just seconds away. But Malefactor's words keep intruding.

What game is that rat playing? Why did he say that about The Swallow? What does he mean? Sherlock can't stop himself. *What significance can there be to the boy being born and raised in Brixton?*

He turns the corner and sees the bulging latticed windows on the front of the apothecary's ancient shop down the street, its brightly colored bottles on display. But the cobwebs obscure them, visible from a long distance – he must clean that up.

He has been longer than he intended. How will he explain this? He approaches the shop and reaches out for the door latch.

Boom!

An explosion sounds at the back, rattling the windows. Sherlock rushes across the reception room's wooden floor and enters the laboratory.

"My boy!" shouts the stooped old man. His face is blackened and his long hair sticks straight out in places, but there's a smile on his face.

"Are you injured, sir?"

"Why, no. I expected a concussion, but not quite what ensued."

Sherlock looks down at the shards of a shattered flask gathered around the Bunsen Lamp on the examining table.

"Methane, acquired from the private area of a cow, held tightly in a flask also containing various chemicals and liquids. I ignited it all . . . and you see the combustible result. Tells me things I need to know about various properties, though."

The apothecary turns to wash his face in the sink. Sherlock surveys the lab. Breakfast is done – his clean mortar and the tea flask sit farther down the table.

"I went out for a morning stroll."

"Did you, now. A long one, I should think."

"Yes, sir."

"Rather a departure for you, is it not?"

"Yes, sir."

"Wanted air . . . isn't that what you said last night too?"

"I . . ."

"I was just about to perambulate myself."

As the old man reaches for his bright-green, tweed frock coat, Sherlock rushes over to help him into it.

"I shan't ask you more about where you went. I am simply pleased you are here. I have outings with three more ladies today." He places his fez hat at an angle on his head. There's another smile on his face – it betrays nothing. He leans forward.

"Women's complaints, but I have just the thing." He utters a characteristic burst of laughter as he waves a sealed vial of a mud-colored liquid in the air.

"The *Telegraph* is here for you. Spot of interesting news that I'm sure you will want to read, about the Crystal Palace . . . uh . . . incident."

He picks up the paper and hands it to the boy with a wink.

"I saw the article," remarks Sherlock softly, smiling back.

"You did?" Bell looks disappointed. "Oh . . . well . . ." he glances up and down the front page, "there are . . . uh . . . other things of the sort you enjoy here . . ." His eyes rest on something farther down the front page. "Oh, yes," he says. "Here's one." He points to the story and holds it up for Sherlock to see. "The Brixton Gang. They've struck again; killed someone this time as well."

The apothecary picks up his huge plaid medical handbag, as big as a portmanteau, and struggles through the narrow laboratory entrance, into the shop's front room, over to the door, and opens it. Noises rush in from the street.

"Keep an eye on things, my page," he barks. The thick wooden door closes with a bang.

The noises are shut out and the old man disappears into the day, off to sit on that bench in Soho Square. There is silence.

But Sigerson Bell's plight isn't on Sherlock's mind now. Something else has lit it up.

The notorious gang is from *Brixton* . . . and so is The Swallow!

9

A CONFESSION

With a stiff straw broom in hand, Sherlock heads for the front window and those cobwebs, thinking. He doesn't have the stomach to deceive Bell again, and has decided that he should stay in and truly clean up the shop. But his mind is on The Swallow.

The borough of Brixton lies between Lambeth, where the young acrobat spent his criminal days, and Sydenham, where the Crystal Palace rules. It isn't particularly large but has been growing of late. Though many of its inhabitants are middle-class suburban folk, there is also an increasing underclass of criminals. London's reigning gang comes from there . . . and so does The Swallow. Do these two facts go together? And if so, what do they have to do with the fall of Monsieur Mercure?

The bell above the front door tinkles before Sherlock can even reach the window, and a man enters. Or at least, his nose does.

"I'm feeling poorly," says the nose.

"You may come in, sir."

Despite the strangeness of this entrance and the rancid smell that is filling the room, Sherlock is pleased. Bell has been averaging perhaps two visitors a week lately, and what they pay him for his poisons has been barely enough to feed them. Perhaps the boy can make a sale. He would sell something to the devil today, if he had to, to help the old man.

The nose, hair billowing out each nostril, looks one way, then another, and finally enters, leading a very thin man with a very small cranium and receding forehead inside. He glances furtively around, and then motions to three others, who follow. They look remarkably alike, all dressed in wet, smelly clothes, black from head to foot, matted hair clinging to their skulls. Sherlock immediately recognizes the dress and attitude of four toshers, who find their living in the sewers and always work in groups so they won't get lost. They search the subterranean arteries of London for prizes, wary of being spotted through the gratings on the streets by pedestrians in the upper world, and of rats, who live in gangs in the underworld, their poisonous bites fatal. A Londoner has to be vigilant indeed to ever see a tosher. Once or twice, Sherlock thought he glimpsed their shadows through a sewer hole, but toshers always darken their lanterns when they near the light.

"Fortune shone upon me today, young man," says the one with the prominent proboscis. "And when we comes up, we is here on this street, and we sees your shop. Have you leeches, sire? Or arsenic?"

"We have both, sir."

"Well, sire, I promised me wife that if I ever found a treasure like this here half-crown, that I would buy her some arsenic, so as to make her cheeks pink." He looks around the room for thieves and then holds out his hand to reveal a silver coin nestled deep in his filthy hand, while the others lean forward to look. "And I also says to meself, I says, Lazarus, get yourself some leeches, sir, and suck the bad blood from your veins."

"He's been feelin' poorly," another tosher squeaks, to remind Sherlock.

"I recall."

"What would you be chargin' for a pinch of arsenic and a bottle of leeches?"

Sigerson Bell doesn't believe in using leeches to suck "bad blood" from the veins of the ill. It is a medieval practice that does more harm than good. But the apothecary does have a bottle of those slimy little devils, swimming in green liquid back in the lab. He only uses them for experimentation. Women, mostly well-to-do ladies, do indeed take poisonous arsenic, sometimes too much of it, to give an alluring glow to their cheeks. But Bell frowns on that too. This is not a sale the old man would make.

"Two shillings," says Sherlock.

Lazarus hands over the half-crown. The boy opens the strongbox behind the counter. There are eight coppers inside. He returns six to the tosher. Moments later, the men slip smiling from the shop with a bottle of leeches and a pinch of arsenic in hand, sliding through the doorway like wafer-thin creatures of the underworld. Sherlock watches them through the window. They look suspiciously up and down the street, pull off a sewer grating, and vanish.

Not long after, as the boy lies awkwardly in the shop window, sweeping the cobwebs away, he turns toward the street and cries out.

A huge face is staring back at him, inches away through the glass. It has black eyes and black eyebrows. Lord Redhorns.

"A message for Mr. Bell," he shouts through the thick window. "Four days. Tell him, that boy. Four days!" Redhorns stomps off down the street, the crowds parting in front of him like the Red Sea did for Moses.

By mid-afternoon, Sherlock has both the front room and the chemical laboratory cleaned up like never before. But he is restless. He can hardly wait for the apothecary to return, and not just because he has polished the half-crown and set it on the examining table for Bell to see, but because he desperately wants to be free to do something about the Mercure case. What, he isn't sure.

He keeps hearing Redhorns' threat.

Four days.

This business about The Swallow's upbringing is tantalizing. But in the end, is it helpful? It just doesn't make sense to him that the young acrobat is involved in the murder. *If he is, why didn't he let me fall from the trapeze perch?* And what could the Brixton Gang possibly have to do with all of this?

Pacing and frustrated, he carefully plucks some books from the precarious stacks and tries to read. Usually these are his moments of greatest joy: with a Charles Dickens novel, a new tract by Darwin, a Richard Francis Burton tale of a far-off land, or the latest Mrs. Henry Wood sensation in his hands. A favorite lately has been Samuel Smiles' *Self-Help*, which puts forth a new belief that Englishmen of any class can achieve nearly anything: it simply takes imagination and especially, hard work. Sherlock loves drifting off into other worlds to feed his mind with information.

But he can't concentrate today.

He makes tea and picks up the *Telegraph* again. He'd only glanced at it in the morning. His eyes fall on "DOINGS AT THE PALACE," on the entertainment pages. This is a short column by a society sort containing a series of single lines about ongoing attractions, upcoming sensations, and statistics. He learns that a balloonist will attempt a leap in something called a parachute over the archery grounds on Wednesday next, that the wonder named *Professor Inferno* will set himself on fire in an "incendiary" return engagement in the central transept, the four-hundred-year-old Californian sequoia tree in the tropical area needs seventeen imperial gallons of water a day . . . and that the writer has heard whispers that money is missing from the Palace vault.

What?

He reads that last line again, the final note in the column, presented sparely, as if the writer has a good source, but no confirmation. As if the authorities are being tight-lipped about it. It is almost as if something doesn't make sense to them, as if the money went missing and, somehow, wasn't noticed. Sherlock has the feeling that there won't be any publicity about this, at least until details become clearer.

But it is evident to him that some time this week the Crystal Palace was robbed.

The bell rings on the shop door again. Sherlock gets to his feet and makes his way into the front room. The possibility of another sale picks up his pace.

Irene Doyle is standing at the counter, her eyes cast down, pretending to be not the least bit interested in his arrival. She isn't dressed like a working-class girl today. She veritably shines in a red silk dress patterned with roses and matching bonnet and shawl. Her blonde hair seems to sparkle and a wonderful scent fills the room. But she looks almost ashamed to be here and Sherlock's heart goes out to her.

"Irene," he says.

She looks up at him hopefully.

He checks himself and his emotions, stiffening his body almost to attention. She notices.

"I'm not here to see you," she says quickly in a hard voice.

"I would be honored if you were."

"Malefactor told me you were living here."

"Something I never mentioned to him," replies Sherlock, looking away.

"He has means to find out."

"He is a rat who feeds off others."

Irene pauses before beginning again.

"He has told me more about himself, you know. He has had a difficult time. His father was a simple dustman in Ireland, picking up rubbish off the Dublin streets. He worked day and night, and made a respectable sum of money, invested in the railroad and increased his wealth dramatically, and moved to northern England. But . . ."

"I do not care what befell him," Sherlock says, cutting her off. "You may have feelings for his sob story, but tragedies befall many of us. I have no interest in him. He is a *rat*." He chews off the last word.

Irene pauses again and closes her eyes, perhaps so she doesn't have to look at him.

"Very well. You have no interest in *most* people, it seems to me, other than those whom you can put in jail in order to make you feel better about yourself."

"I seek justice."

"So do others," Irene counters. "But they don't have to become wooden automatons to do it."

"What are you here for?"

"To purchase something, but my interest has waned."

Sherlock wishes he could make her change her mind. He wonders how much she had planned to spend. But she lifts her nose into the air, turns sharply, and marches toward the door. Before she opens it, he sees her shoulders sag. She turns back to him.

"Can't we be friends, Sherlock?"

He steels himself and answers her with a cold, unemotional face.

The door opens and slams shut.

Sherlock spends the last part of the afternoon pacing in the laboratory, at first trying to keep himself from thinking about Irene, building up a hard resistance to her like a callous over a wound; and then pondering The Swallow anew, wondering about a certain question he asked the boy and the long hesitation in the answer.

The alchemist returns not long after the bells of St. Giles ring five. He has a box full of oysters from the Smithfield Market ready to smoke for their supper, and a pile of little cakes from a Drury Lane muffin-man for sweets after. Sherlock wonders where he found the money – it must be nearly all that he has left. When the old man sees the half-crown, he almost weeps.

Sherlock loves smoked oysters, but he barely enjoys his supper. He gobbles it up, eating as if it were his last meal. He has made up his mind to talk to The Swallow again, and can hardly wait. This time his interview will have a much different tone.

There's a public house named The Faustian Bargain in Leicester Square that music-hall and circus people frequent. Johnny Wilde is sure to be in central London now and certain to be taking meals there. He has nowhere else to be today. The Mercures are out of work until they can hire a new member.

His mouth full of his last two oysters, Sherlock tells Bell he is going out.

"For some air, undoubtedly?"

"Yes, sir."

He accepts a cake from his old friend and eats it on the run, sprinting away into the bustling rush of people heading home from work.

Sure enough, The Swallow is in the public house when Sherlock arrives. He is sitting alone in a booth at the back, a mug of tea and a plate of fish pie in front of him. When he sees the young detective he actually ducks his head for an instant, but then he raises it and waves him over. Sherlock makes his way through the dingy, wood-paneled room, tobacco smoke thick in the air, mixing with the strong smells of beer, coffee, and food. He spots a number of famous faces: sees midget acrobats, recognizes a freak known as the *Animal Boy*, and several comic singers.

"Fancy seeing you 'ere, mate," says The Swallow amiably, with what looks to Sherlock like a forced smile. He motions for Holmes to sit across from him in the booth.

Sherlock sits heavily, keeping his eyes on his target.

"I'm not here for any niceties. You lied to me."

Wilde places both hands on either side of his fish pie. One holds a big steel spoon . . . the other tightly grips a sharp knife. Sherlock sees the boy's knuckles growing white around the handle. He feels adrenaline seeping into his system. The Swallow releases the spoon, picks up the knife and drives it . . . into the wooden table. It stands straight up.

"Yes I did," he says with a sigh.

Sherlock is still recovering from a vision of that knife rising up from the table and being driven into his neck. He can't speak for an instant. But The Swallow can.

"Now you tell me what I lied about, mate . . . because it may be more than one thing."

Sherlock can't help but smile. There is something in the concept of an honest liar that appeals to him.

"I think you know what I am speaking about."

"The question about suspicious blokes loiterin' near us at the Palace before the accident?"

"Yes."

"I was afraid you'd say that."

"How would you answer that question now, knowing that if you don't answer truthfully, I will hand you over to Scotland Yard with the suggestion that you are the chief suspect in the slaying of Monsieur Mercure?"

The Swallow grins.

"Well, knowing what little I know of you, Master 'olmes, graspin' your particular brain power that is more and more evident to me, guessin' that you is in possession of some information about meself that don't look too well for me . . . I would tell you the truth."

"And that truth is?"

The Swallow looks out the grimy little window by the booth. Outside, a narrow alley snakes beside the public house, but it is barely visible through the grime. He rubs the back of his neck with his left hand and sighs.

"There was indeed some folks . . . visitin' me at the Palace the day before the accident."

"From Brixton?"

The Swallow looks away again.

"Yeah, from Brixton," he mutters.

"Of disreputable occupation?"

"I can't give you their names, Master 'olmes. You can turn me over to the Peelers if you like, but I ain't givin' names. There's a sort of honor, you know, among thieves."

"I can imagine," sneers Sherlock.

"I'd wager you can, knowin' the bit I know about you. You have a deadly look about you at times, you do."

He eyes Sherlock and it makes the boy uncomfortable, so he quickly moves the conversation forward.

"Tell me this, just yes or no: were they members of the Brixton Gang?"

The Swallow swallows. No one knows much about the members of that vicious, slippery, and magically efficient group, not even the police. For a moment it seems as if the young acrobat won't answer. He picks up the knife and carves out a slice of his pie, slides it onto the utensil and eats it. Then he looks back at Sherlock, fish evident in his mouth.

"Yes," he says quietly.

The young detective knows instinctively that an enormous piece of this puzzle has just been revealed. But exactly where it fits and what it all means is still a mystery.

"I knew 'em in me youth. Two of the four. They was a bit older 'an me. They is in with some desperate 'uns now. Smaller thieves are useful, can get into places bigger 'uns can't. I don't condone what me old mates do, mind."

He is keeping his head down, as if he were ashamed, eating big chunks of the strong-smelling pie, his jaws grinding the food.

"But you did, one day."

The Swallow looks up at Sherlock, a defiant expression on his face.

"I did. But not now. You can believe me or not. That is up to you, Master 'olmes."

"You can prove it to me."

The Swallow goes back to eating.

"'ow's that?"

"Come with me to the Palace today. I need you to get me in and help me walk about, *everywhere*, without interference. I am guessing that the trapeze apparatus will be removed soon."

"Tonight. I'm supposed to start tearing it down when the Palace closes this evenin'. The other two will be there. I'm takin' the train."

"You shall be departing earlier than you planned and paying my fare."

"With pleasure," snarls the boy with an unpleasant look.

"Eat up," says Sherlock Holmes.

10

THE SCIENCE OF DEDUCTION

A whole new factor has entered the game. Sherlock needs to locate the Crystal Palace vault, *and* see the crime scene one more time before it is dismantled. He has a great deal to discover and put together, and it all must be done in the next few hours.

It is hard to believe that he is going back to Sydenham – he had just been there in the small hours of the morning.

The two boys walk through the Trafalgar Square crowds and approach Charing Cross Railway Station. Its entrance is through a ground-floor arch in an imposing, brick-stone hotel that rises six storeys high. An ornate column with a replica of the medieval Charing Cross at its tip stands in the hotel's forecourt, behind an iron fence. Only the wealthy ever use this building's fashionable two hundred rooms and dining area.

Sherlock tries not to gawk as they move through the arch and merge with the flow of people entering the terminal on the other side. The station's big clock is thirty minutes from striking seven, and many folks are still finding their way home. Though Sherlock appears calm as he walks beside the strutting, loudly-dressed Swallow (who knows how to play his part as he receives stares of recognition), the young detective's mind is racing. He would be ashamed to tell his companion, but he has never once been on a steam locomotive. He is trembling.

Trains move at unimaginable speeds. He had often stopped to watch them explode through Southwark, all power and sound and steam, thundering over the low brick bridges there, built through, and veritably on top of, poor neighborhoods.

The boys pass the W.H. Smith bookstalls that sell nearly every London paper as well as city maps. Gentlemen in top hats rush by, calling out to news vendors, tossing them coins with hardly a glance, and catching their papers.

"*Gazette!*"

"*Times!*"

"*Tely!*"

They hurry, preoccupied, to their trains, reaching into their waistcoats for pocketknives to cut open the sealed pages. Sherlock wishes he had a few coins in his clothes too.

The Swallow buys them two eight-pence, round-trip, third-class day tickets from a uniformed conductor and finds the platform for the South Eastern Railway line to the Crystal Palace six miles away.

First-class cars are elegant and even serve food, but the carriage the two boys enter, solely for the working class, is much plainer. To Sherlock, it is heavenly. He sits down in a wooden seat across from The Swallow and stares out the window. Within minutes the locomotive hisses and chugs out of the terminal, over the Charing Cross Rail and Foot Bridge into Southwark. The boy can feel its power already. They move through Lambeth, along the edge of the river, then to the ancient London Bridge Station. They stop, receive more passengers, and quickly move on, picking up speed as they grunt through rough areas near his old haunts, over those low stone bridges he's so often seen the trains upon. They enter industrial Bermondsey and pass the stinking tanneries on his right, smelling of the lime, rotten eggs, and dog excrement used inside. Then the train swings south, heading into the suburbs and the countryside.

Sherlock cannot believe the speed at which they are moving. It terrifies him. He has heard that locomotives can fly as fast as sixty miles in an hour! He believes it now: his shoulders are pinned back to the seat, his expression held tightly, anxious to look collected in front of The Swallow.

Sherlock has never moved more rapidly than he can run.

The boy looks out his window and straight down, trying to see the tracks, but they are a black stream. Buildings flash past, cows and sheep disappear in the fields the instant they appear. He has always dreamed of being on a train and of taking to the sky in a hot-air balloon, but he never really believed he would get to do such things. Sherlock Holmes wants big experiences. The speed of the train thrills him as much as it frightens him.

But soon he worries that it is out of control. There have been many shocking railway accidents, not the least of which happened two years ago almost to the day on this very line, south of here in Kent, when ten people were killed and many maimed in the notorious Staplehurst crash. Charles Dickens was on that train and the terrifying way he described it in his magazine *All the Year Round* sent shivers down the boy's spine.

As they race south, only minutes out of the London Bridge Station and yet approaching their destination, Sherlock feels the locomotive rock back and forth, barely hanging on. He has to shut his eyes. In his vivid imagination he sees the train flying off the tracks, careering into a field, smashing into a building, and exploding in great red and black flames: he hears the screams of the excursionists, blood splattering the insides of the cars, severed heads and limbs thudding against the windows.

The train slows.

Sherlock opens his eyes. The Swallow is grinning at him.

"Life movin' too fast for you, Master 'olmes?"

The young detective looks out the window, embarrassed, and concentrating on slowing his breathing. The locomotive puffs gently through Forest Hill Station, whistling as it goes, then picks up just a little speed as it enters Upper Sydenham, and the Crystal Palace comes clearly into view. The sun is getting lower in the gray sky, peeking through the clouds. The glass monster glows on its hill right above them.

Sherlock has never seen it from this vantage point. Every time he's been here, even when he came with his mother, he walked. He's always approached the Palace from behind. But tonight the train is taking him past the grounds, and he can see the front of the magnificent building overlooking its green kingdom. The wide Grand Centre Walk leads way up to its tiered terraces and main doors.

The train follows the curving track toward the Palace Station, crossing in front of Boating Lake, populated with little pleasure vessels piloted by gentlemen, with ladies seated in front of them. The Great Fountains are stretched across the width of the park, spurting their white spray high into the sky.

Sherlock disembarks and nearly falls down – his legs are rubbery. A line of elegant hotels runs north from the station, but the two boys take the tunnel onto the grounds and head toward the Palace. The Swallow simply has to show his face to get them inside.

The trapeze apparatus is only one element in the case now. Of almost equal importance is the vault. Sherlock wants to know where it is, and how the Brixton Gang might have robbed it without anyone even noticing, and then deduce what in the world, if anything, all that has to do with the murder of Monsieur Mercure. If that notorious group of thieves indeed played a part in any of this, then Sherlock Holmes will be involved in a much bigger case than he ever imagined. On the surface, it doesn't make sense that all of the factors – The Swallow and the gang from his old neighborhood, the money missing from the vault, and the Mercure accident – are connected. But something inside him says they are. His heart rate increases as he enters the building.

What role did The Swallow have in all of this? Sherlock doesn't trust this self-confident little devil anymore. He marches him up to the central transept. On his way he spots Inspector Lestrade and his son, attended by a half dozen Bobbies, standing at the far end of the nave. They are deep in conversation and look like they intend to stay for a while. Sherlock immediately decides that he must investigate what they are up to, especially why they are gathered in that particular spot, far from the trapeze installation. But first, he has a few more questions for Master Wilde. They lean against a wall near the tower they climbed in the early hours of the morning. Sherlock wants this conversation to take place with the whole scene in front of him.

"Did you ask your Brixton friends to come here the day before the accident?"

"No," answers the young acrobat peevishly. "'Course not. I told you once, I 'ave naught to do with their like now."

"Did you have the sense that they sought you out?"

"Don't know."

"Where did you meet?"

"Right 'ere, where we're standin'. I was puttin' up the equipment."

"So, they saw that you were in charge of the trapeze swings?"

"Suppose they did, yeah."

"Was there anyone else around?"

The boy points across the transept. "Just them two."

The Eagle and The Robin are walking in their direction. They are glancing around, aware that others are noticing them. They pick up their pace when they see The Swallow and the tall, thin boy.

"Stop talkin' to strangers, Johnny, and get to work," the young woman commands as they near. She turns on Sherlock. "Leave off!" she barks.

Despite her nasty attitude, the boy is struck by how beautiful she is up close. Not that she isn't while in the air: her flaming hair flowing as she flies, her face glowing with strong, painted features, and her long muscular legs and slim arms shockingly on display in her almost see-through red costumes; she is always a scandalous and enticing vision, and her entrancing form mixes with the danger of her act and thrills the hearts of every man who has ever gazed up at her.

Sherlock steps back, feeling intimidated.

"I *'ave* to talk to 'im," says The Swallow, looking her square in the face, obviously not afraid of her.

"Why?" asks The Eagle. He steps up close and stands over Sherlock and The Swallow, his size imposing. But Sherlock can see that what El Niño told him is true, just by looking into the man's eyes. The Eagle seems unsure of the authority he is trying to display. Close observation can tell you a great deal about an individual; it can reach into a soul. Sherlock has been trying to rally himself. The other's weakness makes him feel stronger.

"Because I know certain things about the Mercure murder that no one else knows," he says, moving so close to The Eagle that their noses almost touch.

"It . . . it isn't a murder," answers The Eagle, visibly swallowing. "We saw him today. He's still alive."

"That's correct," says The Robin, "and . . ." she hesitates, "what do you know, anyway?"

Sherlock hadn't been surprised to see cracks in The Eagle's exterior, but The Robin looks to be faltering too, her question almost a plea, obviously taken aback by Sherlock's claim. The boy wonders why this brash woman might be frightened. Does she have something to hide? Is she a better suspect than it seems?

"It isn't murder *yet*, you mean," asserts Sherlock. "But the chances are, it will be, and if not, then *attempted* murder, at least."

The Eagle glances at The Robin as if looking for guidance.

"I need more time with your young accomplice," says Sherlock, "so you two may go – for now. I understand you have work to do? Please do not leave the premises until I speak with you."

Always best to leave suspects worrying, he thinks. The Robin and The Eagle, who both seemed to start at the word *accomplice*, leave meekly.

"I had naught to do with this, you know," repeats The Swallow, the instant they are out of earshot.

"Where is the vault?" answers Sherlock dryly, as if he hasn't heard him.

"'ow should I know? That doesn't concern me."

"You know, because you always know where the money is kept at any venue you play. It is in your nature. Am I not correct?"

The Swallow regards Sherlock as if testing his will and receives a stern stare in response.

"It's over there." He is pointing down the nave directly at the police officers. A thought enters the young detective's mind. He is considering a line of investigation that Lestrade, standing directly outside the vault with his son and the constables, has likely never even considered.

"Do you know anyone who works there?"

"Where?"

"At the vault – has anything to do with guarding it?"

The Swallow allows a slight smile.

"I do," he says.

It is the answer Sherlock was hoping for. In fact, he feels as though he has just called the winner at The Derby. The Swallow indeed knows something, and his smile is an indication that Sherlock is getting warmer. Despite the young star's situation, he obviously admires a clever mind.

"Did the guard make the acquaintance of your friends from Brixton the day you met them here?"

"He did."

Sherlock detects a twinkle in The Swallow's eyes now, as if he were inviting his interviewer to ask the right questions. But the twinkle has its limits: the young acrobat also wants to defend himself.

"I will tell you again," he says, "I did naught wrong. I don't know what 'appened that day, I swear on me mother's grave. I'll truthfully answer any question you ask, but I don't want to get no one in trouble, send no one to jail, and I won't volunteer information."

The time has come to ask the right question. Sherlock has the right person in front of him, while the police are lost, as usual.

"Is the guard a young man? Would you say he admires you?"

"'e is, and 'e does, talks to me every time I come 'ere."

"Did he ever tell you anything about his job, brag about it?"

"Yes."

"Did he speak of it that day?"

"Yes."

"What did he say?"

"'e said there'd be one hundred thousand pounds in the vault by two o'clock that day."

Sherlock tries not to show his excitement.

"Anything else?"

"And that 'e keeps the combination for the lock in a notebook in his coat pocket. Said it was very complicated, as though 'e wanted to give us all a sense of 'is importance."

"Us all?" asks Sherlock as soberly as possible. "Who else was party to this *particular* conversation?"

"Two others."

"The members of the Brixton Gang?"

The Swallow is reluctant to answer, but he's promised.

"Yes."

Sherlock is finding it even more difficult to stay calm. He has to keep to his line of questioning.

"Did the guard tell you and your friends anything else of interest?"

"Not really."

"Anything else at all? Trivial matters are sometimes things of immense importance."

The Swallow thinks for a moment.

"I recall that 'e spoke of how much 'e enjoyed the cold lemon drink they make at the Refreshment Department's dinin' room 'ere."

"Did you see the guard again the next day, the day of the accident?"

"I recollect seein' 'im walkin' along the floor of the transept just before I commenced to climb me tower."

"What was he doing?"

"Starin' at me, smilin', steppin' toward the vault."

"Anything unusual about him?"

"No. 'e was just walkin', carryin' a cup o' that lemon drink."

"Did he speak to you?"

"Just waved 'ello, raised the cup to me, mentioned that one of me old Brixton mates bought it for 'im."

Sherlock now has a flock of clues, all flying around in his mind, unconnected. He drifts into one of his characteristic moments of thought, his chin dropping onto his chest, his eyes almost closed, trying to put it all together. The Swallow's voice breaks his concentration.

"I figured me friends might be tryin' to rob the vault, I'll tell you frankly, Master 'olmes. And I didn't interfere. But I tell you again, I did naught wrong. I didn't tell 'em anythin', I didn't help 'em, I didn't gain one farthing from anything they may 'ave done. I am guilty of naught. You're concerned with Mercure, anyway. What does this 'ave to do with 'im?"

It is an excellent question.

"May I go?" pleads The Swallow, "I 'ave all this work to do," he points up at the apparatus.

"Yes, you may," answers Sherlock, "but I forbid you to take down the equipment. Don't remove or lower anything until I tell you that you may. Bear in mind that I still have the means to connect you to this crime. And tell your two accomplices the same. I am sure they did not enjoy their overnight stay at Scotland Yard. I have the power to return them there. You may convey as much to them."

The Swallow has grown to respect the young detective's abilities. He isn't sure what this clever boy knows or doesn't know, but he understands that he shouldn't underestimate him. He nods and heads off toward his fellow acrobats.

Sherlock turns toward Lestrade and the Bobbies and marches directly at them. He isn't going to move on the exterior of this investigation anymore. He is going to enter the lions' den. In the last few minutes, the Mercure problem has begun to unravel. He has a question for the Force, and he is going to ask it straight to their stupid faces. The time has come. He can almost feel the money being placed in his hand. He will present them with his proposition, and then solve this crime . . . right before their eyes.

11

THE ART OF AERIAL OBSERVATION

Inspector Lestrade is taken aback by the sight of young Sherlock Holmes wearing a confident smile. That isn't a good sign. The detective has been examining the area in and around the vault room and is standing outside its door, set in its unusual walls, which don't quite reach the glass ceiling.

"Mr. Lestrade," intones the upstart, as if he were the plainclothes policeman's equal. The Inspector has learned to be suspicious of this lad. This is a boy who knows far too much about everything. But he decides to play along, at least until he discovers whether or not he has anything to gain.

"Master Sherlock Holmes, can I be of any service?"

"As a matter of fact you can. And I can be of greater assistance to you."

A couple of the Bobbies snort and turn their faces away. Young Lestrade steps closer to his father, his face betraying his interest in this conversation. They form a little circle of three.

But Sherlock intends to speak up in a confident voice so that all within earshot can hear. He glances at the room behind the Lestrades, obviously the one that houses the vault.

That's curious, he thinks, the walls don't quite reach the ceiling. For some reason that seems significant to him, but he can't think why, so it passes through his mind and exits.

"I am in a position to make an exchange with you, sir," declares the boy.

"Are you now?" replies Lestrade, tipping his brown billycock hat back and putting his other hand up to his bushy mustache, just in case he is inclined to laugh.

"You tell me one simple fact," announces Sherlock, "which I am guessing you are in possession of, and I shall solve at least one of the two crimes you are investigating."

"*Two* crimes? How kind of you. Didn't know there were two. Which one?"

"The robbery. I know who did it . . . and I shall prove it. All you will have to do is hunt them down. I don't expect a large reward for the information, perhaps fifty pounds?"

This time the Bobbies don't hide their laughter.

But Lestrade would like to hear the boy's theory. He has little intention of giving him what he wants.

"The police are not in the habit of awarding funds to citizens with theories about crimes, real or imagined. If you were indeed to have the information you assert, Scotland Yard might, at the most, find ten pounds for someone such as you."

Sherlock doesn't blink.

"Thirty," he says.

"Twenty would be exorbitant."

"Twenty it is, then." Sherlock hides the excitement bursting inside him. Twenty pounds would both pay for his education this coming term, *and* keep Sigerson Bell in business for another year.

Lestrade wants to get on with this. "What 'simple fact' do you require first?"

"I assume that the guard who was on duty the day of the robbery is in there now?" Sherlock points at the vault room.

"He is."

"Those who handle the Palace funds must check the vault regularly and, therefore, must know almost exactly when they were robbed."

Lestrade clears his throat. "You keep leaping over one point, lad. Who says they were robbed?"

"Come, come now, Lestrade," remarks Holmes airily.

His tone and attitude are almost enough to bring things to a halt. The detective feels like thrashing the boy and sending him on his way. But he knows what remarkable things Sherlock Holmes accomplished concerning the Whitechapel murder and cannot bring himself to miss seeing this little episode to its conclusion.

"Yes, they know when the money disappeared and have told us," admits Lestrade, lowering his voice.

"And when was that, exactly?"

The distinguished policeman now has a decision to make. Should he tell this ragged half-Jew an intimate detail of police business? He is inclined not to.

"Father, I think you sh –" begins his son, sensing his reluctance.

"Silence," says the father.

He again reflects on the Whitechapel murder, how the boy had investigated a vicious killing that didn't have a single witness and pieced together the entire event, uncovering precise details, based on the fact that it was observed in the night by two crows. It really was remarkable. The Inspector also considers the acclaim he had gained from the boy's heroics and how he hadn't had to give him one scrap of credit. Could the boy be as ingenious this time? Unlikely. But what if this brilliant robbery was committed by major stars of the criminal world, and young Sherlock Holmes actually holds the key? The applause, which he could direct entirely to himself, would be deafening. Who would believe that such an invisible minor and a half-breed to boot, was responsible? Lestrade tells himself he is a good man, but one must sometimes resort to darker methods in the cause of what is right.

"Step this way," he says quietly. He leads Sherlock to an area close to the wall, allowing only his son to follow.

"The incident occurred between one o'clock and two on the afternoon of the first day of July," he murmurs.

A thrill goes through Sherlock. The Mercures' show had begun at one. He can't resist a smart response.

"That means the operation began at approximately 1:05."

"How do you –" begins young Lestrade.

"He doesn't!" snaps his father. "Now, what are you going to give me in exchange?" He looks around, "Tell me quietly." He feels a bit ridiculous even asking the boy, but can't resist.

"Bring the guard out and let me ask him a few questions. All shall be revealed."

This is the only way Sherlock can crack the case – he has no other means to make the guard answer his questions. He needs police authority.

Lestrade regards him for a moment. He wonders what the boy is up to.

"We shall not 'bring him out,' as you put it. . . . We shall go in and see him."

It is an irregular thing to do – bring the boy right into the vault room inside a sealed-off police investigation zone – but Lestrade cannot bring himself to have anyone else about when this boy questions the guard. Chances are he will fail and make the Inspector look foolish. But if this minor were to solve the crime out here in front of others, then that would be even worse. Everyone would know. It just wouldn't be right. London cannot have the sense that its safety, the solution to any of it serious crimes, is in the hands and minds of children. Again, one must sometimes use questionable methods to achieve good ends.

"Come with me," says Lestrade, nodding to both Sherlock and his son. He motions to a policeman standing at the vault room door, who opens it and lets them in.

The young guard is sitting on a thick wooden chair, the only piece of furniture in the room. A curtain is drawn in front of the wall to his left, obviously where the vault is built into it. There is a string looping across his chest and attached to a whistle, the top of which can be detected sticking up from his right breast pocket. No one would be able to enter this room without being seen and the alarm being given; the guard could not be attacked from behind; and a Bobbie is always stationed outside the door.

Sherlock looks up. The glass ceiling of the Palace is visible above this room. He notices where the tops of the walls end, a good twenty-five feet below the ceiling. For an instant he glances toward the performance area down the nave. He thought he might be able to see the summits of the Mercures' towers, but can't. The perches must be just below.

Lestrade makes sure the door is closed behind them before he speaks.

"This is Master Sherlock Holmes," he says to the guard. "He has a few questions for you. Anything that is said at this time inside this room is strictly police business and cannot be revealed to anyone at any time in the future. Do you understand?"

"I do," says the young man quietly. Sherlock observes him. A youth of about nineteen or twenty years of age, with sandy hair, the beginnings of a mustache, and bags under his eyes from recent sleeplessness – obviously upset about what has transpired. But his look isn't one of guilt. That worries Sherlock, though he commences his interrogation anyway. His plan is to startle his interviewee and bring him quickly to heel.

"You keep the combination to this vault in your left breast pocket, do you not?" Holmes had seen the whistle in the right pocket.

The young guard is startled by this remarkable opening comment. "Did the police tell –" he begins.

Sherlock cuts him off.

"I have it on good authority that you were in conversation with disreputable individuals in this building on the very day before the robbery and that you told them where the combination is kept."

"I –"

"Do not lie to me. Lying will put you into a deeper hole than you are in now."

The guard hesitates.

"Yes. Yes, I told a couple of people."

Lestrade had been leaning against the vault wall as if bored. He takes a step forward.

"Do you know that I can prove that those strangers were members of the Brixton Gang?"

The guard's eyes bulge. Lestrade steps even closer. His son had been nearer to the action, standing close to Sherlock. His father gently brushes him aside, staring at the young guard.

"Now you must come clean," stresses Sherlock, going for the jugular. "What happened on the day of robbery? Did you let someone in here? Otherwise, how could they enter without being seen?" He pauses dramatically. "Or, did they force their way in, assault you and get away, your shame afterwards preventing you from telling the authorities that it was your loose lips that caused this terrible theft of one hundred thousand pounds?"

Sherlock doesn't know exactly what happened. But he is speaking aggressively, sure that this will shake the young man and cause him to reveal what he knows. And what he knows will unlock everything. The details of the daring robbery are about to be heard.

But the guard surprises him.

"No!" he asserts with confidence. "No one came in here. I will swear to it on a Bible. There was no robbery! I don't know why money is missing from the vault. I was here the entire time. Nothing happened!"

"Are you quite finished?" asks Lestrade glaring at Holmes and stepping between the two.

"No . . . I –" stumbles Sherlock.

"I think you are," shoots back the Inspector. "This young man," he points at the guard, "has told us everything we have asked of him. And everything he has said turns out to be the gospel truth. We knew he bragged a bit too much about his job to others – he is hiding nothing from us. He comes from a respectable family with money invested in the Palace, a place from which he will one day profit. He certainly wishes it no harm. His home has been searched and so has his bank account. You are dead wrong about everything, Master Holmes. I suggest you leave and don't come back. If I see you on these grounds, I shall have you forcibly removed . . . or perhaps horsewhipped!"

"There was robbery here," sputters Sherlock. "It commenced at 1:05 on the first instant of July. It was committed by the Brixton Gang. And it is connected to the murder of Monsieur Mercure."

"How?" demands Lestrade, holding back a smile.

"I . . . I don't know that part yet."

"I see."

"But, if you allow me, I can make it so you can lay your hands on both the murderer and every member of the Brixton Gang."

"The idea that this apparent robbery" spits the detective, "was committed unseen by the most notorious gang in London and that a flying trapeze accident nearly a fifth of a mile away is somehow connected is a fantasy: the fantasy of a child involved in something well beyond his powers to comprehend!"

Lestrade glowers at him.

"You are wasting my valuable time. If you do not leave this second, boy, I will lay the hands of the Force on *you* and have you thrown into The Boating Lake."

Sherlock's face is burning. He has made a terrible mistake. He has gotten ahead of himself, grown too excited, believed he had the facts when he didn't, depended on another to reveal things about which he was not absolutely certain. There is no substitute for cold, dispassionate reasoning, and in the excitement that had followed his last interview with The Swallow, he had forgotten that.

"Twenty pounds!" mutters Lestrade, stalking away.

Sherlock's head and leaves droops as a Bobbie escorts him down the nave, depositing him near the front entrance with explicit instructions to leave the premises, along with a promise of what will be done to him if he does not. The sun is setting, darkness is descending. The fireworks will begin soon.

The moment the policeman leaves him, the boy darts back from the entrance, disappears into the crowd, and reenters the Palace. He is *not* giving up. He will get the money. He must.

The Swallow and his two colleagues don't know that Sherlock has just been thrown out by the police. They are still wary of him and what he might be able to do to them: The Swallow because of what the young detective has demonstrated he knows and the others, because they are all too aware that they may still be looked upon as suspects by the police. If they have indeed escaped the clutches of the law, they want it to be permanent. Sherlock can still make those three do his bidding. That is a card he can continue to play. But what can he do with it? He may only have a few hours left: the apparatus must be taken down soon and the Mercures may be allowed to leave London in the very near future. All evidence, already gathered and yet to be found, may soon be gone.

He makes himself invisible as he moves through the crowd back to the central transept. From his spot behind a big white statue of Prince Albert near the amphitheater, he can see that the police are still hovering near the vault room.

His mind is searching desperately, going back over what he knows, examining where he made mistakes, what he has missed.

What has he observed today that he hasn't thought through yet? Often commonplace things, little details assumed not to be important at first, are the most valuable of all. Any scientist will tell you that. Have there been any recurring facts, observations he's made more than once?

Something occurs to him.

Several times today, he's noticed the strange fact that the vault-room walls do not reach the ceiling; and when he was inside that room with the Lestrades, he had observed it again and looked up to see if he could spot the tops of the trapeze towers. But it seems like a frivolous detail, not related in any way to the crime . . . or is it?

Sigerson Bell is fond of telling him that one can trace every human thought to a clear motivation. People don't just think things. One's mind always has a reason for going (or even wandering) in the direction it does, even if it doesn't seem that way on the surface. For some reason, Sherlock's mind had twice considered those unusual walls.

"Our instincts," the old man likes to say, "are often ahead of our brains. We know something, but don't realize it. I try to tap into that instinct when I diagnose a disease. Sometimes, something in the back of your brain, or shall we say, your gut, tells you what the problem is."

Why does Sherlock keep noticing the short walls of the vault room?

He slouches against the pedestal beneath the statue and sighs. As he does, he looks up at the perch from which he nearly fell in the small hours of the morning, remembering the terror of it all. For an instant, he can't stop himself from reliving it.

He shoots out over the transept on the flying trapeze, feeling as though his life is about to end. He recalls looking down . . . and noticing a room *with walls that didn't quite reach the ceiling.*

That was the first time it had occurred to him. He concentrates on what he saw. What had it meant to him? Why, afterwards, did he keep noticing it? Suddenly . . . he realizes what it is.

He could almost see *inside* the vault room from the apex of his swing on the flying trapeze! No other vantage point in the Crystal Palace affords such a view. None! He thinks of Monsieur Mercure and how incredibly high he soared that day.

Sherlock stands up and darts through the crowd to the base of the tower. The Swallow is loitering there.

"Master 'olmes," he says, "can we tear this down yet?"

"No," says Sherlock excitedly, "not yet. Do you want to absolve yourself entirely of this crime?"

The expression on the other boy's face grows serious.

"I do."

"Then climb up that tower, get on the trapeze, and swing as high as you possibly can, as high as Mercure usually went."

The Swallow looks at the boy as if he were a lunatic. No one is expecting a performance, and the boy is dressed in his street clothes.

"'e always went the 'ighest," he finally says, as if delaying.

"I know. Do this for both of us, Johnny. And when you do, look toward the area where the police are gathered, toward the room they are standing in front of, where the vault is, and tell me what you see."

The Swallow climbs the tower, ascending as quickly and silently as a mouse. He reaches the perch, grabs the swing, and sends himself flying out over the central transept.

Down below, several people notice. There are *oohs* and *ahs* and soon hundreds, then thousands, are looking up, pointing to the distant glass ceiling. The Swallow swings very high, then pumps his legs and goes higher and higher, approaching maximum speed, thrilling the crowd. They begin to applaud. Finally, he alights back on his perch, landing to a great roar.

At the bottom of the tower, The Swallow is met by Crystal Palace officials and two Bobbies, angrily asking him why he was up on the apparatus. Clever as always, he insists that it is a flying trapeze tradition to do this before the "tear-down." While they are discussing whether or not to believe him, he slips away and finds Sherlock.

"Well?" the young detective asks, a look of anticipation on his face.

"I could see right into the room, Master 'olmes. I could see the far wall with the curtain drawn across it and I could see the guard sitting there in 'is chair, as plain as day."

Sherlock smiles.

"It has been a pleasure to know you, Master Wilde," he says. "You are a gentleman and a star. You may go and so may your two colleagues. Break a leg."

The Swallow grins back. "Much obliged, sir. The pleasure 'as been mutual."

Sherlock Holmes walks straight out into an open area where the police can see him clearly. Lestrade notices, his face turns red and he yells for a Bobbie to pursue the boy. Sherlock drifts into the crowd again, the policeman after him. Young Lestrade watches with a look of wonder and slight admiration.

The tall, thin boy steps down the big front staircase of the Palace under his own steam with that smile still on his face. The grounds glow, lit by their many gaslights, and up above, fireworks explode in loud concussions and marvelous colors in the black sky.

Only Sherlock Holmes knows what Mercure said just before he fell. And now he knows what it meant.

"*. . . silence . . . me.*"

Le Coq wasn't saying that he knew that the silence of death was descending upon him. No, he was trying to tell Sherlock something! High in the air, he had just witnessed a robbery. He was the *only* one who could see it. The thieves had known long before they committed their crime that that would be the case. As part of an ingenious and complicated plan, Monsieur Mercure had been instantly and expertly removed.

In a horrific moment of realization, the trapeze star had been trying to tell Sherlock Holmes that these fiends had *silenced* him.

HOW IT WAS DONE

Sigerson Bell knows. Under that red fez, below that balding pate with its yellowing strings of long greasy hair, inside that bulb-tipped skull, his always-thinking, always-questioning big brain has been following the mental and physical moves of the admirable young Sherlock Holmes. And enjoying it. Amidst his troubles, this boy is such a gift! The old man is blessed with the powers of deduction of an astute medical man and alchemist and is used to diagnosing patients at a glance. Thus, he observed Sherlock's interest in the Mercure incident in the *Daily Telegraph*, put that together with the fact that the boy's father worked at the Crystal Palace, that he was gone for precisely four hours and twenty-six minutes on the very afternoon of the accident – an appropriate time to get to Sydenham and back – and that a small shard of unusually colored purple wood was embedded in the decaying toe of his left Wellington shoe, obviously the remnants of Le Coq's splintered trapeze bar. This brought him to the elementary conclusion that Sherlock Holmes had not only been at the Palace and witnessed the accident, but had been very close to it indeed.

The boy's demeanor since then: his barely contained excitement, his questions about brain concussions and circus performers, his extended absences, even in the middle of the night (when Sherlock had slipped out to break into the Palace, Bell had crouched at the top of his spiral stairs in the darkness, listening to the boy's movements down below), had convinced him that Master Holmes was pursuing the case. He knew of the lad's interest in crime, something of his past, and had gleaned his connection to the solution of the Whitechapel murder during their many conversations. If the truth be told, the old man was absolutely thrilled about it all – it was like dining on filet mignon and Yorkshire pudding before being hanged. Adventure was afoot! Evil had taken place! And *his* young boarder, a youthful knight crusading for good, was in the middle of it all, right on the trail.

What he did not know was that the boy was also planning to save his life.

Though it is growing very late, the apothecary hasn't gone to bed. Instead, he is just sitting down to perform an aria from *The Magic Flute* on his valuable Stradivarius violin, purchased at a bargain long ago from a nearby Jewish pawnbroker. He always plays it in an unusual position on his knee. But when he hears Sherlock Holmes returning, he sets it down quickly. He knows the sound of the violin makes the boy sad – it was the instrument his mother loved.

Sherlock is whistling a merry tune, his mind obviously deeply engaged in something. Bell can't stand it anymore. He is desperate to be involved.

"I must ask you where you have been," he says as he moves to a tall stool at the high examining table in the lab, where minutes earlier he had been mixing a green gooey alkaloid and the pulverized heart of a bat. The smell is rather off-putting.

Sherlock has just taken off his coat and placed it on a hook, ready to clean up this latest mess before he goes off to bed. He stops abruptly and ceases whistling. Bell is looking at him over the top of his glasses, which have slid down to the tip of his red nose, nestling at the knob that resides there in all its vein-filled glory. The old man has never asked him anything like this.

"Uh . . ." replies Sherlock. Best to tell some version of the truth, he decides, the old man is no fool. "I was at the Crystal Palace . . . to see my father again. Did you need me? I apologize if . . ."

"Master Holmes," sighs Bell with a smile, "I am not a devil from the Spanish Inquisition, nor do I wish to follow or control your every movement. You may do as you please so long as your chores are completed. And I believe they are."

Sherlock smiles back, feeling relieved. But instead of looking away, the old man keeps smiling at him. It is rather unnerving. The boy attempts to go about his duties. He picks up a rag, wets it in a pail of water, and begins to wipe the counters and containers. But no matter where he goes, even when he is behind the old man, he has the sense that that smile, those watery red eyes, are still trained on him. Finally, the old man speaks.

"Why don't you tell me about it? Perhaps I could be of some use?"

"About what?" asks Sherlock, fixing the most innocent look he can muster onto his face.

"Come, come now, Master Holmes."

Sherlock then knows that Sigerson Bell knows. He should have guessed long ago. How could anyone keep something from this brilliant old man? But the boy doesn't want to share what he's learned about the Mercure incident: he wants to think about it on his own. All of the elements of a solution are at hand – the facts are spinning in his brain. He simply needs to fit all of these pieces together, something he has been trying to do since he left the Crystal Palace nearly an hour ago. He wants to see the crime as Mercure saw it. If he can just . . .

"Sometimes, you know," adds the glowing old man, "two heads are better than one."

Sherlock indeed needs another brain. And what a piece of tomato aspic sits under that red fez hat: a teeming blob of cranial jelly capable of helping him line up all his clues, and see the crime exactly as it occurred. He certainly doesn't want to ask Malefactor for advice, and Irene, despite her intelligence, is out of the question.

But how can he bring someone he cares for into something like this? The last time he did, Irene was nearly crippled for life . . . and his mother was killed.

He looks at the kindly old man, the only adult friend in his life now. He can't do this to him.

"I shall be in no danger," states Sigerson Bell. It is a startling thing to say, as if he were a spiritualist reading Sherlock's thoughts as clearly as the headlines in the *Daily Telegraph*.

"I . . . I have hurt people in the past," sputters the boy. He hasn't shared his feelings like this since before his mother died.

"I am an old man, Master Holmes. I *love* adventure and intrigue. Were I to even *die* helping you do something like this, I would expire with a smile upon my face. I would never regret it."

It reminds Sherlock of what his mother said not long before she was killed.

"But . . ."

"I shall likely kick the proverbial bucket soon anyway, my boy. Now, tell me about this. I will help."

Sherlock hesitates. He doesn't want the old man in any danger, whether he is on his last legs or not. His plan is to save him, not kill him. And deep inside, he is suspicious of *anyone's* interest in his endeavors, even Bell. Why is the apothecary *so* intrigued?

"I live in a locked building in the center of London, far from any of this," continues Bell, stating his case as clearly as a Lincoln Inn's Field magistrate. "None of the devils involved in this would have any reason to do anything to me."

Sherlock's need to solve the crime is about to get the better of him. With a little help, the solution to the infamous Mercure incident could be at hand.

"Tell me," repeats Bell earnestly.

And so the boy does.

They sit together on the two high stools at the table in the laboratory as Sherlock tells him what he knows: a disjointed story with disconnected but tantalizing facts. When he is finished, the apothecary ponders it all with a look of abiding intrigue, elbows on the table, face cupped on either side with his hands. He and the boy sit silently for a few moments. Finally, the old man speaks.

"They used a sedative potion on the guard," he says clearly.

"Who?"

"The Brixton Gang."

That is a major missing piece – in fact, it makes the whole crime possible. Instantly, Sherlock begins to see what Mercure saw. He is high above the Crystal Palace on performance day, dressed in his royal purple tights, Le Coq, the magnificent master of The Flying Mercures. He grips the purple trapeze bar and swoops out over the central transept, a monster crowd gathered below. The bar feels a little shaky for some reason, but he pays it little heed – it is show time. He is a catcher: the one who will catch and throw the smaller flyers. But his first maneuver – one that always thrills audiences – is to fly himself, as high as he possibly can, using his great experience and enormous strength to stun spectators with his speed and elevation. It will be especially sensational here in this magnificent Palace. One swing, two, three . . . he reaches his apex. From up here the view is remarkable. *But what is that?* Almost directly in front of him in that room with the walls that don't quite reach the ceiling: a man is slumped on a chair and two others stand in front of a vault, their heads turned to look up for an instant toward the performance. Then the trapeze bar snaps at both ends and he is falling, dropping like a bird shot from the sky. He screams. Looking down, he sees a dark-haired boy dressed in a tattered black frock coat and waistcoat, wearing Wellington shoes. He is heading directly toward him.

The apothecary's voice brings Sherlock back to the laboratory.

"What we have is a superficial view of this crime: a theory, with holes in it. We must now examine what happened in detail, from start to finish, and most importantly, we must understand *how* it happened. Let us piece it together, out loud. Tell it to me again, adding the information I contributed about the sedative, and I will try to help you when you reach gaps."

"The members of the Brixton Gang," Sherlock begins, his eyes staring into the distance, his fingertips drumming against one another, "are so clever that their identities aren't known to the police. They were casing the Crystal Palace in broad daylight, undetected, the day before the accident, already well aware of where the vault was and the different ways they might get at it. They were deciding on the best approach, in search of the key to another perfect crime. Then everything fell into their lap."

"They meet their old friend, now known to the world as The Swallow," nods Bell.

"They know he won't give them away," continues Sherlock. "So they start to converse, asking him innocent questions about the performances, learning that Le Coq flies by far the highest, that he nearly touches the glass ceiling . . . that he would be able to see into the vault room."

"That seems like a problem for them, at first," notes Bell.

"But then the guard, who worships The Swallow, who stops whenever he can to talk, comes along. He is introduced. The Brixton boys hide their immediate interest and slip into their quiet technique of drawing information out of others by asking innocuous questions. Soon the guard is bragging about the fact that there will be a great deal of money in the vault by tomorrow afternoon, at least a hundred thousand pounds. He also states that he keeps the combination to the lock in a notebook in his breast pocket. Before he leaves, he tells them something else: he loves the delicious lemon drink one can purchase in the Refreshment Department nearby."

"A beverage into which one might slip a helpful potion," adds Sigerson Bell, turning and writing a few chemical symbols on his little chalk board on the wall.

Sherlock looks at it. He understands almost everything now.

"The Brixton Gang knows a great deal about poisons and medicinal mixtures," adds the alchemist sadly. "The use of them, as well as the gang's elusiveness, love of misdirection, and murderous ways during robberies, are all trademarks of their nefarious operations."

"They leave the Palace," says Sherlock, "come back with an appropriate tool of their trade, and later that day, one of them distracts The Swallow just as he is finishing his work on the trapeze bars before they are raised to the perch . . . and the other slices two cuts at the ends of Mercure's swing, each about halfway through it, and perhaps camouflages them with paint.

So, the scene is set for one of their perfect crimes. The four members of the Brixton Gang arrive at the Crystal Palace early on the day of the event. They mix with a large and growing crowd drawn by the promise of a marvelous flying trapeze performance, and situate themselves near the vault room's door, which is undoubtedly always guarded by a Bobbie or two, likely bearing concealed revolvers."

"But there is a sensational performance about to begin just down the transept," chimes in Bell, "an irresistible show the Bobbies will be able to view from their spot outside the door."

"When the band strikes up, their attention shifts down the transept." Sherlock looks at Bell who nods. "The world-renowned Flying Mercures are about to perform."

"Still, the policemen are professionals and keep an eye on the door," cautions the apothecary.

Sherlock thinks for a moment. Then he has it. "But, when Le Coq himself seizes the trapeze bar on his lofty perch and the drumroll begins, it is too much for the policemen. It would be for anyone. They stare away, up into the distance."

"And thus the Brixton Gang strikes. They spring the latch on the vault-room door with quick and ghostly expertise."

"In all probability, two go in and two remain just outside."

"Inside, the guard doesn't see them, because he is slumped on his chair, his half-finished cup of lemon drink gripped sleepily in his hands, drugged into a stupor."

"They remove the notebook (with the combination) from the guard's pocket, open the vault, and take the money."

"And return the little volume to its sleeping owner," adds the old man.

"And while they are doing this, a terrible accident occurs down the transept. It transfixes everyone, including the Bobbies. No one can take their eyes from it. Le Coq screams, he falls like an anvil toward the hard floor and strikes it with a sickening thud. Pandemonium ensues. Everyone rushes to the fallen man. There is deafening noise, shrieks and wails, women fainting, absolute confusion in the Palace. The Bobbies outside the vault-room door are caught up in the crush, and are either pulled along by it, away from the door, or simply stunned. Who would not be? The door behind is of no interest to them for at least a minute."

"But from that door now sneak two villains dragging sacks of money. They are met by two others. With smiles on their faces they move against the crowd, the other way, out the big rear entrance of the central transept and to a carriage with fleet horses nearby. They are gone within minutes."

"Behind them the vault-room door is shut and locked, as if it had never been opened."

"Their perfect crime is complete, made possible by brilliant misdirection: by the Bobbies' interest in the trapeze performance, and cinched by the accident."

"The policemen have no reason to inspect the vault room. Within half an hour, the guard slowly rouses, unaware that anyone has been in the room."

"In fact, no one even knows that the Palace has been robbed."

"The gang is long gone. There is just one witness . . . and he is dead. *Silenced.*"

The two irregular, amateur detectives had been speaking faster and faster, and have come to a sudden halt.

"There are several potions they could have used," says Bell. "Laudanum with a few drops of chloroform would do nicely. It would mix transparently into the opaque lemon liquid and render a human being insensible for at least half an hour. You would rouse with the sense that you had simply nodded off for an instant."

Sherlock starts to pace.

"What will you do next?" asks Bell excitedly. "To Scotland Yard with the evidence?"

"No."

"But why not?"

"There are many reasons. Firstly, even though we *know* we are correct, to them this will all just sound like a theory. I acted too rashly before. What does this give them, really, even if they believe it? The Brixton Gang is gone, vanished again. To the police, simply knowing that these fiends committed this crime is almost worse than not knowing. If they tell the public the truth, they will look like the fools they are . . . another case of the Brixton wizards outsmarting the Force, this time killing a great performer and disappearing into the night. And in addition to everything else, I will be the bearer of the news. Inspector Lestrade doesn't like that . . . at all."

"But I could come with you. I would do that, my boy. Right down to Whitehall! I shall back you up!" The old man shouts his last sentence at the top of his lungs and turns to a battered old painting of Queen Victoria, hanging on the wall, barely observable through test tubes and glass phials. He actually clicks his heels to attention. He can see it now: in his last few failing days, just before he must tell the boy that his world has fallen apart, he can do something wonderful.

Sherlock smiles, but then his face grows dark. His eyes narrow. "No," he mutters. He paces rapidly back and forth across the lab again, sweat dripping down his face. "It isn't enough. I will go one further. . . . I will capture the Brixton Gang myself! Every last one of them. . . . I shall lay my hands upon these villains."

Five hundred pounds of British sterling are gleaming in his mind.

PART TWO

THE BRIXTON GANG

"I have heard, Mr. Holmes, that you can see deeply into the manifold wickedness of the human heart."

– A client in *The Adventure of the Speckled Band*

I KNOW SOMEONE WHO KNOWS SOMEONE

It is an ambitious, intoxicating idea, and exceedingly dangerous. But what if Sherlock Holmes could actually deliver the notorious Brixton Gang, the most violent, most wanted collection of villains in all of London, into the hands of Scotland Yard? He could fund his education forever, save Sigerson Bell, truly begin his attack on crime . . . and Lestrade would not be able to deny him his due.

"That is not feasible!" blurts out the old alchemist, getting to his feet and making several little circles around the boy. "How could you possibly do such a thing? The Brixton Gang members are not only frighteningly brutal in their manner, *murderers*, but they are as elusive as phantoms. They have disappeared again. The police have no idea who they are, let alone where they are. No one does!"

"I know someone who just might know something," says Sherlock and he springs to his feet, swipes his coat from the hook, and heads out the door.

"Master Holmes, it is nearing midnight!" cries the old man. "I . . . I shan't keep you if you . . ." But the boy is gone.

He has been on his feet since the early hours of the morning. If he persists much longer, he will have spent an entire day pursuing the case. But that doesn't matter – he hardly thinks of it. There are fiends to catch and the time to strike is now. The prize is irresistible. Alert for his prey, he sweeps along streets lit by the soft yellow glow of gaslights, heading into the bowels of the city. The fog is heavy in the humid night.

If it were his choice, he would have nothing more to do with Malefactor. But events are compelling him in the young crime lord's direction. He needs him. Whatever must be done to succeed, to bring those culprits to justice, shall be done. Sherlock will sign a deal with the devil if he must.

The master criminal had been near St. Martin's Workhouse just off Trafalgar Square earlier in the day, so the boy starts off in that direction. Shadowy Lincoln's Inn Fields can be searched later if necessary.

He sees ragged beggars, brightly dressed and painted women, drunk men, and the shoeless, pale-skinned poor, either staggering about or creeping along in the yellow fog, but no matter where he looks, he cannot find Malefactor. The shadows are hiding him well tonight.

But rounding a corner off St. Martin's Lane he spies someone else: the Irregulars' most disgusting operator, hard at work. Nasty, dark-haired Grimsby, dressed completely in black with his face charcoaled too, and hatless, is toiling in tandem with a younger thief tonight. The smaller boy is more nattily attired: cleaned up as best as possible, a tattered greatcoat fitting loosely on his boney frame. They have been out hunting and have spotted an easy mark: a gentleman in evening dress, silk white scarf around his neck, black top hat on his graying head, elegantly mustached, but obviously confused, and more than a little lost as he shambles about trying to go westward toward his wealthy neighborhood, but heading north.

"Hansom cab? Cabbie? Why can't a gentleman find a driver!" he shouts in a slurred voice.

The younger thief, standing next to a Horse and Carriage Repository where vehicles are built and kept, beckons him to approach. Several carriages are gathered around in its small yard behind a black iron fence, some unfinished. To the man's inebriated brain, this must look like an enormous cab stand.

"Cab, guvna?" shouts the little Irregular. "Stand 'ere and I'll bring one along, sir."

Sherlock slides up against a building. He can see Grimsby crouching in the lane that runs to the front doors of the Repository. He is hidden from view, ready to pounce, and shaking his fist at another group of boys, not Irregulars, who have obviously also been following the gentleman. He is letting them know that this is not their prize tonight.

The gentleman sways toward the younger Irregular and then reaches into his pocket for a coin, turning his back to the entrance to the lane. Grimsby shuffles into perfect position from behind and suddenly drives forward, striking his victim violently in the back of the knees with his shoulder, knocking him, face down, onto the cobblestones. The man groans. The next blow comes from the hard toe of the boy's boot driven against the gentleman's head. This time the man goes limp. Grimsby and his accomplice pull him into the lane, go through his pockets, strip him to his undergarments, and make off through the streets with his clothes and money, running low to the ground.

"To your heels!" he hears Grimsby hiss.

Sherlock is after them in a flash. It had pained him to watch them operate. He had wanted to shout out, stop them in their tracks, save that man from them. But he couldn't: he had to watch it all transpire so he could follow them when they were finished. He has larger prey to ensnare. Allow a crime in order to end greater evil – it is the price he has to pay.

"Speed, you vermin! Speed!" spits Grimsby under his breath.

They are scurrying north-east, human rats on the run. Sherlock keeps low and stays on their trail, following them past a smelly brewery, a church, a school, and then the hospital near the Bloomsbury and St. Giles Workhouse. They are heading to a spot in a poor neighborhood . . . not far from where Irene Doyle lives in the more genteel Bloomsbury area, a fact not lost on Sherlock.

They turn up Drury Lane and slither down a little mews that leads right onto the workhouse grounds. This dark "house," one of many feared by the poor, who are put in these places when they can no longer survive on their own, is a big, granite building. It is silent now, its desperate, ill-nourished inmates asleep, or tossing and turning on their hard little beds.

Sherlock sees Malefactor instantly. He always stands out from his gang. He is leaning against the cool, stone workhouse wall in his tailcoat and top hat, twirling his walking stick in anticipation of Grimsby's return. When he spots Sherlock, he scowls angrily at his lead lieutenant, who, as the mob's thief extraordinaire, should have known that he was being followed. The young boss turns to the other, smaller thief, knocks the gentleman's rich garments from his hands, and drives the end of his cane deep into the little boy's ribs, eliciting a shriek of pain. Somehow the lad ducks the ensuing blow, directed at his cheekbone. Malefactor pivots and glares at Grimsby again, who slinks away into the shadows, looking daggers at Holmes. The gang's other lieutenant: blond, silent Crew, grins nearby.

"Master Sherlock Holmes, I perceive," Malefactor growls, his dark, sunken eyes turning to the boy, trying not to betray his anger. "I see you have returned to my presence." There is an undertone of interest in his voice, as if he had hoped that Sherlock would come back some time.

"Intriguing location," says Holmes, looking about. "Bloomsbury is to your taste these days?"

"Unquestionably," smiles Malefactor.

"I –"

"She often comes to see me."

"Who?" asks Sherlock.

Malefactor merely snorts.

There is a long silence. The criminal knows why Sherlock is here and is forcing him to speak first, shaming him. He examines his fingernails.

"I . . ." begins Sherlock.

"Yes?"

"I need some information."

"Let me quote you, Master Holmes, upon the occasion of your last interview with me. '*I don't need help from the likes of you anymore.*' It was said with some mustard in your tone. I believe I have that correct, do I not?"

Sherlock hates this, but he must endure it. At first he doesn't reply.

"Do I not?" repeats Malefactor.

"Yes."

"I did not hear you." He is cupping an ear in one of his white-gloved hands.

"Yes!"

"Thank you. Now, what brings you here? For what, specifically, are you groveling now?"

"I am after the Brixton Gang."

Malefactor says nothing at first. Then he laughs so loudly that it seems he may wake all the inmates of the Bloomsbury and St. Giles Workhouse. And almost instantly there is a chorus joining in, lead by Grimsby and the others – Crew, as usual is mute, though his smile, visible in the shadows, is cheek-splitting.

"I know they killed Monsieur Mercure!" shouts Sherlock.

It brings the laughter to a halt.

"Perhaps you should announce that on the top of Nelson's Column at Trafalgar Square," says Malefactor quietly. "Even if it isn't a fiction, keep your gob shut about it!"

"It is true. And I intend to lay my hands upon them and bring them to justice for it."

The crime boss looks at him closely, saying nothing.

"They planned his murder," continues Sherlock through his teeth, "and robbed The Crystal Palace of one hundred thousand pounds simultaneously, in a crime of misdirection. They took the money from the vault and left a locked room behind."

Crew takes a coin from his pocket, places it in the palm of his hand, showing it to the other boys. He points at the coin, closes his hand over it, then opens the palm to reveal that it is empty. In a smooth move, he swirls the other hand in front of his chest and opens it . . . revealing the coin.

"Misdirection," mutters Grimsby.

Sherlock ignores both of them. "If it helps me get what I want," he offers, "I shall tell you *exactly* how they did it."

Malefactor appears to be considering this. Information is, to him, like gold, especially information about the activities of other members of the criminal world. He understands that Sherlock wants to exchange it for something. His eyes shift about as he thinks. A chess game has begun. This time, he intends to win.

"No thank you," he responds.

The boy finds this surprising. And Malefactor has a strange look too, a sort of poker-face set on his features, as if he were trying to keep his thoughts concealed. *What is he thinking? Why did he refuse?*

"Give me something else," the young boss says, eyeing Sherlock as if he were looking into him. The boy has the feeling that Malefactor is checking to see his reaction to the refusal, to see if it is giving anything away.

Sherlock wonders what else he can possibly offer. He looks around the workhouse grounds and his eyes glance north momentarily toward Bloomsbury . . . Montague Street . . . and Irene Doyle. He must be dispassionate about this, thrust aside all his emotions . . . all his feelings.

"I shall no longer stand between you and Irene. If you want her friendship, I shall not discourage her. I shall speak highly of the way you have helped me. And I shall give you any further information I gain about these villains."

Malefactor's eyes narrow. Behind him, both Grimsby and Crew are shaking their heads. Would their boss really give up information about the dangerous Brixton Gang simply to impress a young lady? It would put them all in peril.

"You would hand her over to the dark side?" inquiries Malefactor.

"That is not how I would put it."

"Nevertheless."

The taller boy paces, his heavy, black boots crunching the bits of sand and gravel on the cobblestones. Then he stops and strolls over to Sherlock, coming to within a few inches of his face. His appearance is disconcerting: his face radiant in the dim gaslight, his eyes glowing as if he has an idea that thrills him. His minions gather closer to hear what he will say. But he speaks softly.

"I know someone who knows someone who knows whom you seek. His name is Dante. He is stunted in growth . . . one of his ears was torn off in a tussle with a butcher's boy at a dog-and-rat fight last year. You shall find him in The Seven Dials. Do not speak to him. Mention me at your immense peril. I wish you luck."

Malefactor's face suddenly darkens. If there is such a thing as evil in an expression, it is there in his – his eyes are dead. A cold chill runs down Sherlock's spine. He is seldom truly afraid of the other boy, but feels that way now. He finds himself speechless. He merely turns and walks away, not looking back. Behind him, Grimsby is protesting and Malefactor is calming him. He soothes them all with a few words. Whatever he says makes them laugh. Sherlock can hear Grimsby's malicious giggle above the others.

He returns to the apothecary's home still feeling frightened. Malefactor has put him onto a scent that may lead him right to the most brutal men in England. Why did the young criminal do it? And why with such relish?

His employer is fast asleep, snoring so loudly up above that it almost shakes the building. Sherlock doesn't try to wake him. He crawls into his bed in the chemical laboratory and leaves him in peace.

A DANGEROUS TRAIL

"I should like to go for a stroll, sir, if I may, beginning late this afternoon. I might not return for supper."

Sigerson Bell knows what Sherlock means. And he isn't happy about it. Seeking the Mercure solution is one thing, dealing with London's murderous, reigning gang is entirely something else. He and the boy are sitting in the laboratory taking another of their unique bachelor breakfasts: tea and headcheese this time, the latter speared upon their scalpels.

The apothecary thinks for a moment. He adjusts his red fez on his stringy white hair.

"If you must do this, I shall only give you permission if you promise me that, whilst you are on your *stroll*, you will not approach anyone in the Brixton Gang or anyone connected with them without an officer of the law attending you."

"I promise," says Sherlock instantly.

"A promise involves one's honor, my boy. To break it is disgraceful."

"Yes, sir."

"You may leave early then."

Holmes is in The Seven Dials the instant he is set free. It doesn't take him long to spot the stunted, one-eared boy. Dante is dressed in a ragged red shirt and red trousers and sports a bowler hat on his head. While Sherlock watches and swelters in his dark clothes in the oppressive afternoon heat, the boy snakes up and down the seven narrow streets that emanate from the middle of the Dials like spokes on a wheel. He speaks to several dozen people, often secretively exchanging small items for coins, looking about as he does. Sherlock sits on a rotting wooden bench, under a statue, pretending to read the *Daily Telegraph*. He shifts his gaze each time the boy goes down another little artery, observing him as though he were sitting in the center of a clock, his view the hands, and the boy various numbers. He could swear that the lad spots him several times, in fact looks right at him, almost as if to be sure that he is being observed. But the rascal never approaches him or attempts to fly away. The swarms of poor folk buzz about in their dull soot-stained clothing. In order to be inconspicuous, Sherlock twice gets up and leaves, but each time he returns to his watch, he easily spots the colorfully dressed boy, still making his rounds in the neighborhood. Eventually the lamplighters arrive and the sun begins to set.

Dante makes his move. In an instant Sherlock is off his bench and following. The one-eared boy darts down White Lion Street and heads through Covent Garden near the Opera House (where Sherlock used to crouch outside with his dear mother to listen to the swirling violins), and on like a thoroughbred rodent toward the river. He turns east at The Strand, apparently anxious to stay on the busiest streets, vanishing and materializing in the thick masses like an escape artist. He is making sure that no one is following. Or is he? At times it seems as though he is checking to be certain that Sherlock is on his trail.

They walk for what feels like an hour, and throughout the entire time Sherlock Holmes suspects that he is being followed too. If he is, it is expertly done, because every time he turns he cannot spot anyone in pursuit. Dante goes all the way to the old city, through it, and into the East End. It isn't an area where Sherlock wants to be. It's where Lillie Irving was murdered in the little lane north of Whitechapel Road, where he came several times to investigate her gruesome death – once with Irene, other times alone in the dead of night.

Working-class people, returning home, dominate the wide street. Jewish old-clothes salesmen who ply the trade his poor grandfather once pursued, trudge past with hats piled high on their heads, glancing at him with distant looks of recognition. He passes a street named Goulston, then sees Old Yard off to his left. *That's where it happened.* He can't even look that direction: remembering its narrow darkness, the poor children lying on its foot pavements, and the lane where all that blood . . .

Dante veers and Sherlock follows. At first he fears they are heading for Lime House, the area southeast of the Thames where the scariest parts of Mr. Dickens' latest novel are set, where perhaps the roughest, most violent men in all of London live – those who make their living from the docks and the river. If he is indeed being led toward the haunt of the Brixton Gang, this area would be perfect. But Dante goes straight south instead, through poor residential neighborhoods with dirty little brick houses packed together along many small winding streets. This is a bad parish too, but Sherlock keeps his wits about him, ready in case he is pounced upon. He wishes he knew more about defending himself.

Several times, he thinks he loses the scurrying boy in the red clothes, but the lad keeps reappearing, far ahead on narrow cobblestone roadways like a tattered fox still in view of the hunt. Behind Sherlock, another hunter seems to keep following, but when Holmes looks again, no one is apparent. Soon they are at the London Docks, where giant British ships are built, or simply loaded. From here they make for Canada, India, the Orient – the world.

There isn't much activity this time of the evening, just the sounds of a few men working, cursing, and grunting as they struggle with heavy cargo loads in the night.

Is this Dante's destination? Could the Brixton Gang be holed up on a ship? Do they make their escapes by sea?

Ahead, the one-eared fox stops. He looks back. Sherlock ducks down behind a big wooden crate. He peers through its cracks and sees that someone has come out of the shadows and is approaching, a figure just a little taller, dressed in black, apparently wearing a frock coat and tattered top hat. They talk in hushed tones for a moment.

Sherlock wonders if this might actually be a member of the Brixton Gang. His heart rate increases. The sweat drips from his face to his clothes. He must get nearer. He needs to hear what they are saying, know exactly where his prey is lodged.

Just as he rises, the two figures part, moving in opposite directions. Quickly! Whom should he follow?

"I know someone who knows someone who knows whom you seek." That's what Malefactor had said.

He chooses the second figure.

This one moves even faster. At times Sherlock has to run. That means taking more chances. He glances back again to make sure that no one is pursuing, and sees shadows flitting about in the darkness, hears sounds – perhaps just the rustlings of the big cat-sized rats that live here. He presses on. Before long they are almost on the banks of the river.

Then the dark figure does something surprising. He rushes up to the doors of an octagonal, marble building. It is the entrance to the Thames Tunnel that runs under the brown river to industrial Rotherhithe on the south side. The world's first underwater tunnel, it was a tourist attraction in the past, with shops down its descending stairs, along some of its thirteen-hundred-foot length, and up the ascent on the other side. But lately things haven't been going well: folks fear for their safety inside these days – the shops are not as numerous or respectable as they once were, thugs loiter in the vacated alcoves, robbing victims who dare to enter alone. A few months ago, it was purchased by a railroad company, and shut down this very week to investigate the laying of tracks.

Up ahead the dark young figure is doing something to the latch of one of the great doors with a knife of some sort. He toils for an instant and then slips inside. It seems foolhardy to approach. That boy has a weapon. And what if Sherlock has been spotted? This would be a perfect place for someone to wait in hiding, and attack him.

Holmes crouches outside the building for a while, not knowing what to do. But he can't wait for long. He has to decide. He thinks of Sigerson Bell sitting alone and distraught in Soho Square, of the five hundred pounds that would change their lives.

Sherlock rises and approaches the door. It obviously had been locked, but then pried open and . . . left slightly ajar, just a crack, as if inviting him to follow.

He grasps the door with a trembling hand . . . and opens it. It creaks. He slides in and drops to the floor. The sound of the door closing echoes in the big rotunda. But it's the only sound he hears.

There's no one in here.

He's heard stories about this place being haunted – many men died when it was being built, buried under collapsing soil or horribly drowned in an inescapable underwater underworld.

There are a few dim gaslights left on. The rotunda is impressive, at least fifty feet across, walls lined with deserted vendors' stalls, a little ghost town of sorts. Across the round room sits a cage for the penny-ticket collector and a turnstile, abandoned too. Sherlock, with his long legs, steps over its iron spindles. In front of him is a set of steps leading downward. What awaits him in that hell below?

His legs feel like jelly. He approaches the stairs nervously and starts down. At the bottom of this first flight another flight descends the opposite way, then another, and another. He is dropping deep below the River Thames. The air is hot and thick down here.

Up above he hears a sound . . . like someone entering the building and walking across the rotunda!

What if they have him in a trap, one brute in front and the other behind? It would be a perfect maneuver. No one goes after the Brixton Gang and comes out alive. Another terrifying thought passes through his mind. Is this Malefactor's doing? Is this why he had that strange look on his face – the evil expression? Has he been drawing his rival in these last few days, setting him up for this? Sherlock remembers how quickly Malefactor's words had calmed Grimsby, how the bloodthirsty lieutenant had laughed. Malefactor is not to be trusted . . . he could easily want Sherlock dead.

He turns to face whoever is coming down the stairs, but there are no footsteps anymore. *Is* it the ghost of the Thames Tunnel?

He stands still near the bottom of the last flight, holding his breath. Still, no one comes out of the dimly lit space above. He reminds himself of the prey he is pursuing. He turns and scurries toward the tunnel.

Before him is a dirty, gray-bricked archway about six or seven body lengths across with a high ceiling. In its heyday, its alcoves were filled with shops and other enticements, even ladies telling you your future by reading the palms of your hands. But today everything is dank and empty. Sherlock hesitates at the entrance – he can't hear the dark-dressed boy anywhere, yet this *must* be where he went. It is pitch-black up ahead: Sherlock can't see through to the other side. He takes a deep breath and starts to run, his footfalls echoing. The sounds reverberate and multiply. It seems to him that they are coming from up ahead too . . . and from *behind.* He stops suddenly, his chest heaving. The sounds continue to echo and then fade.

BOOM BOOM . . . Boom Boom . . . boom boom.

Silence.

He is near the middle of the tunnel now and there is nothing but curving dark walls in the gloom around him and the only sounds are his own breathing. When he begins running again he hears those footfalls once more. He stops again. They stop.

Is there someone up there? Behind?

Several strides later the gloom turns to utter darkness. Sherlock stops running and walks carefully, his hands stretched out in front of him, into black.

He feels something. A human face!

He screams.

It screams.

"Who are you!!!" it shouts. It's an old woman's voice. His hand has gone into her mouth and feels her toothless gums.

Sherlock pulls away and begins to run as hard as he can, his stomach burning, heart pounding, sprinting in complete darkness, not knowing if he will run face-forward into another vagrant human being, a wall, a ghost, or a murderer. But he doesn't care; he has no choice but to move. It is a strange sensation, fleeing into nothing, as if there is no guidance in life, no God nor parents – nothing except blind fear. He wants there to be some form again, some idea of where he is going. . . . For some reason he prays for a sense of right and wrong.

Eventually, the tunnel lightens a little and before long, he can see the dim way out at the far end. He heads for it like a racehorse seeing the finishing line at The Derby. He doesn't even think about the boy he is pursuing – he just wants to get to the light.

There is no one in the building at the other end, a near replica of the one on the north side. He climbs the marble steps carefully and quietly, his fear finally beginning to recede.

The grand doors in the big rotunda are locked from the outside but open easily from inside. He steps out into the humid July London air and hears the sounds of the river – steamers chugging gently, men's voices shouting in the distance. This is an industrial area, filled with factories, warehouses, and dominated by the Grand Surrey Docks. There aren't many gaslights. There are few people about and any that are, will be tough characters indeed. The black-looking Thames, punctured here and there by its many wharves and gray stone stairs, is still and ominous. The Surrey Gas Works are behind him, a flour mill down at the water. The many pools, timber yards, and offices of the Docks surround him.

Sherlock sees no one at first. Where has the dark figure with the knife gone? Does he *really* want to find him?

But then he spots the lad, a few hundred yards away, stepping out from behind the corner of a big brown building topped with a crowd of chimney stacks and marked with a huge dirty sign reading BEELZEBUB'S BISCUIT FACTORY. It is curious. Again, Sherlock has the sense that his prey actually showed himself on purpose, that he glanced back to make sure he was observable before he slithered away.

Holmes follows. The boy heads up cobble-stoned Rotherhithe Street which runs next to the Thames, winding along the river's Lower Pool in the direction of Lime House, before it turns down the peninsula toward the Isle of Dogs. The very sound of those names frightens Sherlock. It is a witheringly dangerous area, absolutely fit for the likes of the Brixton Gang. He is descending into London's darkest place.

Sherlock can smell the big chemical works nearby, the filth and grease in the tanneries. He passes the Surrey Dock Tavern, and then the Queen's Head Inn, containing the only signs of human life, with glowing windows in run-down wooden buildings, filled with drunken shrieks and laughter.

Somewhere near here, thinks Sherlock, *brutal Bill Sikes had been pursued by the Force, accidentally hanging himself on a rooftop in front of a bloodthirsty mob in Mr. Dickens' frightening novel,* Oliver Twist. That chapter had always scared the liver out of the boy, but he had loved it too. . . . He doesn't now. He has no desire to meet a real-life ruffian like that. The reality of confronting the members of the Brixton Gang is looming in his imagination.

The boy with the knife slows his pace. He is approaching the Whiting Asphalte Works, a grimy, sprawling factory with massive black smokestacks. Across from it sits a series of warehouses that look like they are falling down as they lean against one another, the whole lot about to crumble.

Sherlock hears a sound behind him and turns to see a shadowy figure, obviously a boy, moving swiftly toward him along a narrow lane. *He is caught; just as he feared; between the two lads in the night.* He looks at the one with the knife and sees him turn back as if making his mind up about something. *He, too, is coming in Sherlock's direction.* They are closing in on him. He can't see either face. There is but one option: flee! He can only get away if he runs as hard as he possibly can, back the way he came, on Rotherhithe Street. If he doesn't fly this instant, the boy coming up that lane will get to the street first and intercept him. He is sure the Brixton Gang is nearby, but he can't stay a second longer: he must scramble for his life.

He takes to his heels at top speed, churning up the distance, shoes whacking the cobblestones. If either of these two roughs catch him, they will surely kill him.

Sherlock darts past the lane, not even looking toward the boy, and is gone. He doesn't bother with the tunnel and runs until he gets all the way to London Bridge. He scrambles along its old stone surface without breaking stride. He thinks he can feel at least one pursuer close behind, but can't take time to look. Back in the City proper on the north side, he follows every small artery he can, winding and swerving his way through central London. It is a long trip, but even when he finally nears Bell's dwelling, his pursuer isn't shaken. Sherlock scoots along the footpath near the buildings on Denmark Street and then pauses outside the shop door, hears footsteps nearing, and runs again. Deep in The Seven Dials he finds an alley where he can hide.

Many hours later, as the sun is rising, he makes his way back to the apothecary. As he enters the front part of the shop, fear fills his stomach like a vat of chemicals dumped from a boiling cauldron. The lights are on in the laboratory but there is no sound . . . *absolutely* none. It is an eerie silence. Thinking about how he had stupidly led whomever was pursuing him right to the very door of his old friend's home and about his dear mother's death, he rushes into the lab, his heart pounding.

Sigerson Bell is lying on the floor. And he isn't moving.

15

SUSPECTING MALEFACTOR

Sherlock drops to his knees and collapses beside the old man. He is numb. Life is over for him. Why had he believed that he, a poor half-Jew, a child really, could gain this reward, battle evil . . . make a difference in the world?

Then he hears a noise beside him.

It sounds like someone getting to his feet.

"My boy?" asks Sigerson Bell. "Are you not well?"

"W-what?" stammers Sherlock, rolling onto his side and looking out of a teary eye. He sees the old man gazing down at him, trying to place his fez back on his head, a little wobbly on his legs, but very much alive, an expression of concern on his face. He is holding a damp handkerchief in one hand, and it smells.

"I thought you were . . . were . . ." says Sherlock.

"What?"

"Were . . ."

"A dinosaur? A dog with seven legs? An extremely handsome man for my age? What?"

"Dead."

"Dead!" shouts Bell, looking momentarily petrified. "I don't think so." He feels his heart, his jugular artery, his rear end. "Oh . . . oh . . . I see," he exclaims, glancing down at the spot where he had been lying motionless on the floor.

"It was an experiment," he explains sheepishly.

Sigerson Bell likes to take his own medicine, as it were.

"I have been fascinated for some time, as you know," he continues, "with the effects of chloroform on the nervous system of Homo sapiens. Dr. John Snow, the esteemed physician to the queen and perspicacious seer into the true cause of typhoid and consumption and the like, uses it during every child-birthing he attends. One pours it on a cloth and holds it to the nasal apertures. Women experience no pain whatsoever, even though God decrees they must in Genesis . . . which is hogwash!"

Sherlock sits up on the floor.

"You gave yourself . . . chloroform? How much?"

Bell looks guiltily down at the rag.

"A substantial amount, I fear, my boy. Wanted to see what it felt like firsthand. It is a good thing to know. I wonder how long I was unconscious? It felt disturbingly good, I must confess. One could even grow to like it." He arrests his smile and scowls at his listener. "Addiction, my boy, is an evil thing!"

Sherlock leaps to his feet and hugs the old man who responds by growing as stiff as the knifeboards on the top of the city's omnibuses. Then he gently pats the lad on the back.

"Come, come, now Master Holmes, I am fine. And I am glad to see that you are too. You did not return at all last night." He wags a finger at the boy.

"No, I didn't, sir."

"Where you in Brixton?"

"No sir, Rotherhithe."

Sigerson Bell looks shocked. It certainly isn't the sort of neighborhood he would advise young Sherlock Holmes to frequent.

"Well, I am not pleased about this, not at all."

"I am sorry, sir."

"Were you accompanied by an officer of the law?"

"I didn't draw close, sir, I promise. I merely investigated."

The old man regards the lad for a moment.

"I shan't pursue the significance of the word *merely* nor the past tense of *investigate* as employed upon your lips just now. But I shall caution you to be careful. Should you go again . . . the Force should be with you!"

Sherlock nods, two fingers on his right hand crossed behind his back.

Lord Redhorns had given the apothecary four days. The boy hadn't told the old man. Bell is aware that an ax is about to come down upon his neck, but he isn't exactly sure when. Sherlock knows: there are just forty-eight hours left.

He must go back to Rotherhithe tonight. And he must

go *completely* alone. All he needs to do is confirm where the Brixton Gang is holed up, just see them with his own two eyes. Then he can make his way quickly to Scotland Yard in Whitehall and tell the authorities. But there will be conditions asked of the police: he will reveal nothing to them until they all get to Rotherhithe. He will demand that a member of the press accompany them – he doubts Lestrade will be able to refuse even this. No one, not the senior detective or anyone else, will take the credit due Sherlock this time. No one will be able to deny him his reward.

But first, he must make sure that he isn't followed. That is of paramount importance.

He tries to sleep a little in his wardrobe but can't. His mind is racing. He must get moving. But first, he has to tend to his chores.

"Master Holmes," says Bell before the chimes of St. Giles strike five, "have you noted that you placed the bat urine in my extra hat, poured the strychnine poison into the flasks from which we drink, and threw the dust from the floors into a retort and placed it in the ice-box? Your mind, shall we say, is not exactly riveted upon your work."

"Uh, no sir, it isn't."

"I am listening to the gods, and getting the message, foretelling as it were, that you would . . . like to go for a stroll. Have I erred?"

"No, sir."

Moments later, he is out the door, racing for Montague Street. There was indeed only one person who knew he would pursue the Brixton Gang last night; only one who told him to follow a certain someone . . . only one who could have entrapped him.

Malefactor.

Was his rival's intention murder? Would he actually have him killed?

It is time for a confrontation unlike any they have ever had. If Sherlock wants to succeed in this case, he has to make the young villain back off. Another trip like last night's could be lethal. Tonight's investigation must take place under perfect conditions.

He doubts that Malefactor will be anywhere he might be expected today. The snake will be avoiding him, will have slithered into one of his holes for a while. But Sherlock is guessing that he visits Montague Street almost daily, whether he sees Irene at home or not – the crook finds the princess irresistible. Malefactor knows that Sherlock has taken a vow to stay away from the girl in order to protect her from danger. The young thief lord, therefore, won't expect him to be on this very street. Sherlock has also promised that he won't stand between Malefactor and Irene. But that doesn't matter anymore – his rival is obviously not the man of honor he claims to be, something that Sherlock never should have believed in first place.

Sherlock hides himself behind the stone steps that lead to an unused door on the east side of the Museum. He is completely hidden and yet commands a view of the Doyle home across the street. He gazes over at the long windows behind the flower boxes. Figures move inside. A slim, golden-haired one makes Sherlock sad . . . so he exerts all his energy and deadens the feeling.

It doesn't take long for the street fiends to make their appearance. First to materialize is Grimsby. Sherlock spies him instantly from his vantage point: only the rascal's head and neck are in view, topped by his crushed-in black bowler. He bends around the corner by a gas-lamp, seeing if the coast is clear. The nasty little head vanishes, then pops out again. Within a few seconds, three figures turn up the street, Grimsby and Crew and their boss. The two ruffians look like royal guards escorting their criminal king. Malefactor obviously doesn't trust any other members of the Irregulars to accompany him near Irene's house; no one else is allowed to know that he has any tender feelings, that he needs a friend, an angel. They cross the street so they won't pass directly in front of her home and head up the foot pavement . . . toward Sherlock. They are all acting nonchalant, but their leader glances over at the Doyle home every few strides to see if he might catch a glimpse of her.

Sherlock coils himself into a ball and presses his back against the steps. He is a good ten feet from the road, behind a wrought-iron fence and open gate, mostly out of view.

The three scoundrels pass.

Sherlock stands and follows them. He says nothing. It is almost comical. But suddenly the three in front stop.

"Sherlock Holmes, I perceive," says Malefactor in a deadened tone without turning around. Then he pivots and walks back down the street, passing Holmes without even looking at him. There is nothing remotely like guilt on his face. Once past, he picks up his pace.

"You have some explaining to do!" shouts Sherlock, the anger he has been holding back beginning to rise.

Instantly, he feels a sharp pain in the back of his legs and falls face forward onto the footpath, losing most of the air in his lungs and almost smashing his teeth into the hard surface. Grimsby's shoulder has taken him down as surely as it floored that drunken gentleman in the night. Sherlock remembers what came next; a blow to the temple. Somehow, he rolls quickly over onto the street and staggers to his feet. When he looks at Grimsby, his foot is indeed poised to strike. Blond Crew stands silently nearby, a kind of cold, dead calm in his blue eyes. Sherlock doesn't trust either of them not to maim him for life. They are both sadistic and violent.

"You don't speak to the leader like that, Jew-boy!" hisses Grimsby, a vein popping out on his forehead as his face turns red.

Sherlock glances down the street where Malefactor is moving away at top speed, crossing the street as he goes, heading south, his long black coattails and the back of his top hat in view. Holmes barely hesitates: he springs forward and makes for him, walking quickly, immediately feeling the other two breathing down his neck.

"Follow him if you choose, mongrel," whispers Grimsby into his ear, "but you won't 'ave your 'ealth by the end of the street."

Sherlock knows he means it. He is scared but keeps following. If he can just get close enough to Malefactor, maybe he can make him talk. The other two boys will likely hurt him whether he stands or runs.

But there is a little lane that juts off Montague Street a few dwellings before it reaches Great Russell Street. As Sherlock nears it, both lads seize him. They drag him down the lane and into a little mews that runs parallel to the road along the rear of the houses. Sherlock sees the back of the Doyle house several dwellings to the north. Now he is *very* scared.

Grimsby begins to beat him, while Crew, dressed all in brown today, stands guard, smiling. Resisting will likely make them angrier and Sherlock cannot fight both of them. He takes the blows from fists and feet, trying his best to shield himself, desperate to do something but not sure what.

Grimsby seems to have something wrapped around his knuckles, like a piece of iron. He speaks as he works, spitting out his words. Sherlock is in the hands of a bully far worse than any ever seen in a schoolyard. Like all those bullies, he has demons; his anger comes from his fears.

"You think you're better than me, don't you? . . . You think the boss respects you more? Think . . . I'm . . . a . . . Jew? . . . I'll . . . show . . . you!"

"MALEFACTOR!" screams Sherlock, finally hitting on what to do. "YOU'RE A COWARD!"

It works, thank God. It isn't something Malefactor can stand to hear, especially on Montague Street.

"Cease," says the young chief quietly through clenched teeth. He had returned from Great Russell Street, and had been standing at the edge of the mews, just around the corner out of sight, listening to the beating.

Sherlock gets up. His ribs ache and there is blood at the corner of his mouth, but he raises himself to his full height and stands as erect as he can despite the pain. Then he turns to Malefactor, whose face is red.

"I am no coward," he snarls, smoothing out his tail-coat and using every effort of will to contain his rage. "I am a knight of the streets. You wouldn't understand my kind of honor."

"Then speak to me . . . and call off these piglets." Sherlock is gasping for air.

The roughs glare at him. Malefactor waves for them to stand back.

"I shall decide if this is to continue," he pronounces, "depending on what you have to say. But I must warn you that your chances are not good." He examines his finger-nails for flaws.

"Your *honor*? Do you call it honorable to trap me in a dangerous part of London, to turn my life over to villains?"

"Who says I did?"

"Me."

"And you are an expert, no doubt."

"Is that not why you are avoiding me today?"

"I want nothing to do with you, especially now."

"Frightened of something, are we, Sir Galahad?"

Malefactor clenches a fist.

"Anyone disturbing the Brixton Gang in any way will be removed . . . from life," he growls. "We all respect that. If you choose to pursue them, then you are a grievous liability . . . not just to them but to anyone who knows you, including me. Do not whine about it. You have made your bed, now lie in it!"

He nods to Grimsby and Crew.

"Take your medicine!" adds Malefactor as he turns to exit the lane.

But not a single hand is laid upon Sherlock Holmes. In fact, everyone freezes, though Malefactor looks like he might melt.

Irene Doyle is standing at the entrance to the lane dressed in a white silk dress, a white bonnet tied with flowered laces on her head.

"I heard a shout," she says quietly.

Malefactor snaps around and holds a hand up to Grimsby and Crew.

"What is happening here?" she asks, looking at Sherlock's face, an expression of pain crossing her own. She takes a few steps toward him.

"He fell down, Miss Doyle," says Malefactor, "and we were helping him." He moves between her and Holmes.

Irene is unconvinced but doesn't resist. She looks back and forth between the two tall boys. The three of them standing in this triangle are a lonely trio, each desperate for friendship, but caught up in life's circumstances. Irene knows that gentleness can solve all this. Her eyes plead with Sherlock's, but he steels himself and looks away.

She takes Malefactor by the hand. Holmes steps forward and almost cries out. But he stops himself and stands still.

"Thank you for being so kind," Irene says to the young dark knight, but her eyes are watering.

"This gentleman," spits Sherlock, pointing a stiff, accusing finger at Malefactor and backing away from the others while nearing the entrance to the street, "was just telling me about his sense of honor."

Malefactor bows.

"He said I wouldn't understand it. I wonder if you would, Miss Doyle?"

She gently removes her hand from Malefactor's and says nothing.

"I have one question for him before I leave," adds Sherlock, taking a few more steps toward the street, still warily facing the ruffians. "I want to ask this, straight out. Did you have me trailed last night, and will you have me trailed again?"

Malefactor looks from Irene to Sherlock. Then he regards his enemy with a deathly stare.

"Such things are mysteries," he says coldly.

Sherlock turns to leave.

"You know what they say about playing with fire, Master Holmes," adds Malefactor. He reaches out and takes one of Miss Doyle's gloved hands and kisses it. She can't resist a smile.

Sherlock walks away. No one follows. They wouldn't dare chase him in Irene's presence. He wishes he could go back, wrench her from that devil's grasp and escort her safely home. But he can't. He has bigger fish to fry . . . in Rotherhithe.

16

BELL'S SOLUTION

Sherlock Holmes doesn't know how he will do it. He walks back to Denmark Street puzzling over his problem. He's gained no assurance that Malefactor isn't plotting against him and doesn't know if others are onto him either. How can he get from here to those crumbling Rotherhithe warehouses without being detected and trailed? And then there's the potentially more dangerous problem of how he will confirm that the Brixton Gang is actually in one of those buildings. But he must take one difficulty at a time.

He enters the apothecary's shop.

"Attack!" Bell screams from the lab. Sherlock rushes through the reception room to see the stooped alchemist and a well-dressed woman in a respectable, mauve bonnet, facing one of the skeletons that hangs on a nail in the lab. The woman is approaching it stealthily. She lifts her dress slightly and gives the bone-man a tap with her foot. Bell sighs.

"With all due respect, Mrs. Hawkins, that would not do much harm to a wood fairy. No, no, no. I want you to attack this villain. Look at the way he leers at us! Observe."

He takes up his walking stick, pivots, and turns upon

another skeleton. With his feet splayed in a wide stance, somehow perfectly balanced despite his crooked frame, he wields the stick like a sword, confronting an enemy. He thrusts it forward, parrying first and then smacking the skeleton with an alarming blow as he shouts an equally alarming oriental word at the top of his lungs.

"*KI-AI!*"

Then he closes in on his target, releases the stick, allowing it to clatter on the floor, and seizes the skeleton in a complicated grip. From that position he sweeps one of his legs forward to knock his skinny combatant to the floor. He takes the boney fiend down hard, with an elbow dug into its neck. In an instant, he springs back to his feet and turns to Mrs. Hawkins.

"Now, I want to see that sort of evil attitude in *your* combat, though you shall do it as you are attired, sans the walking stick. A lady would not be carrying one, would she? I have taught you the technical skill, the maneuver, but I want to see *attitude*! You must identify his tender regions and strike them without mercy! ATTACK!"

The lady lifts up her dress to a shocking height, almost to knee level, feints one way with one foot and then drives the other deep into the skeleton's crotch. Her opponent's entire hipbone shatters and it falls into a heap on the floor.

"Excellent, Mrs. Hawkins! Tender regions be gone!"

But the smile on her face doesn't last long. As she turns, she spots a tall, dark-haired boy watching from the lab doorway. Her face turns crimson as she drops her dress.

"Sherlock!" exclaims Bell. "May I introduce Mrs. Hawkins."

"I . . . I was assaulted in Soho Square," she explains, "or nearly so. This kind old gentleman came to my rescue. He . . . knocked the man unconscious."

"Merely doing what anyone would do."

"He is teaching me how to defend myself."

The boy has seen the alchemist hard at this sort of endeavor before, but never with a pupil. It is the defensive art of something Bell calls *Bellitsu,* which he has often invited Sherlock to learn. The boy-apprentice has always politely declined, but lately has been wondering if he should at least give it a try. Feeling the Grimsby-inflicted bruises on his face (which he can't hide as he stands there), he thinks of how helpful it might be to become the master of such an art.

"I once knew a customer, boils I believe he had," the apothecary explained the first time this subject surfaced, "who spent two decades working as an engineer in the oriental country of Japan. There he learned the ancient Far Eastern secrets of fighting, grappling, and striking – martial arts – more specifically jujutsu and judo. Always interested in physical activity and called upon to visit patients in neighborhoods of less than salubrious variety, I was intrigued. Once he was well, I asked him to teach me his secrets. We spent many days in a local gymnasium beating the stuffing out of each other. It was grand! To these two Japanese arts, I melded the Swiss craft of stick-fighting and England's own gentlemanly sport of pugilism to create the alloy I call . . .

Bellitsu! It is adaptable to any situation: the use of the cane or umbrella at just beyond arms' length, boxing in slightly nearer, and the oriental arts for combat at close quarters!"

Mrs. Hawkins reaches into the thick folds of her mauve-colored dress and takes out her coin purse. She snaps it open.

"No, no," says Bell, holding up a hand.

"But I must pay you."

"No, you must not. It was my pleasure, especially should what you have learned from your humble servant allow you to defend yourself with vigor some future day on the streets of this fair city."

"Sir," says Sherlock, "perhaps you should let . . ."

"Your face!" exclaims the old man, really looking at the boy for the first time.

Bell quickly and kindly ushers the woman from the shop, still refusing the money, and scurries back into the lab.

The old man gapes at the boy, then starts pacing, looking back at him from time to time. "You must reveal all to me!" he shouts, his stringy white hair flying and his spectacles almost falling off that bulbous red-tip at the end of his nose, as he shakes his head. "You are most evidently in growing danger!"

"I have another problem," confesses Sherlock. There is no one he can speak to who is wiser than this old man. If anyone can come to Sherlock's aid, he can. "I need your help."

A smile spreads across Bell's face.

"We shall concoct a solution!" he cries, then pauses. "Always minding what I said about having the Force with you. We shall plan nothing reckless!"

The apothecary listens carefully as Sherlock explains his situation. Then he drops dramatically into a flea-bitten old armchair in which he likes to ponder medical problems. His head sinks down onto his chest and his eyes appear to roll up into his head. But within minutes he has sprung to his feet again.

"We shall disguise you as Sigerson Bell!" he exclaims.

"We will do what?" asks Sherlock.

"You and I are about the same height, my boy. I am stooped, caused by the calcification of the lumbar vertebrae and lack of proper exercising of the latissimus dorsi muscles at the appropriate age."

He stops to ponder this thought for a moment and appears to slip into the contemplation of long-gone activities.

"Sir?"

Bell and his brain jump back into the summer of 1867.

"Yes!" he exclaims. "Yes! Yourself in the character of one Sigerson Bell Esquire. Here we go!"

He turns and climbs his spiral staircase. Soon Sherlock hears all sorts of noise emanating from above: pots and pans appear to be rattling, heavy cases thumping on the floor, apparently the sound of glass shattering . . . Sherlock even thinks he hears some sort of animal growl. A few moments later Bell thuds down the stairs carrying more things in his hands, on his head, and even expertly balanced on his thighs than a dray horse could carry in a wagon. He deposits them all with a crash on the floor in front of the boy.

"Here we are!" he shouts. "Where shall we begin? I am considering not only dressing you in an exact replica of what I would wear for an evening's consultation, but also designing a new nose for you to match mine and . . ."

"Sir?" interrupts Sherlock.

"Yes, my boy?"

"I think we need to simplify. Whomever might follow me will be doing so from a distance. He will be identifying me simply by my clothing. I doubt there is a need for the creation of an entirely new nose."

"Ah!" says Bell, fingering his own substantial, red-tipped proboscis. He looks disappointed. "I suppose you are correct."

He reaches in amongst the pile of clothing and pulls out three items: a dusty, green greatcoat very much like the one he wears to see patients, an older version of his red fez, and a battered black medical bag.

"How about these rags?"

"Perfect," smiles Sherlock.

He will leave in a few hours. They spend the day together, trying to work. But it is difficult for either of them to concentrate. They are waiting for the sun to set. As it finally grows dark inside, Bell rushes around lighting gas lamps on the walls and a few candles on tables, muttering to himself about exactly how the clothes will be placed on

Sherlock and little touches he might add. Meanwhile, the boy has slumped down into the arm chair, his fingertips playing on each other, deep in thought.

The apothecary can't wait any longer.

"Are your ready, Master Holmes?" he asks, looking even more frenetic and nervous than usual.

Sherlock stands up. As he does, he realizes that his hands are even sweatier than they should be in this terrible heat wave.

Bell retrieves the coat, the hat, and the medical bag, placing the first around the boy's shoulders, the second on his head, and handing him the last. Then he fusses with all three: adjusting the hat many times, trying different angles, wondering for brief silent moments about how he wears the same, lifting the coat's collar up to hide the boy's hair, smoothing it down, turning the handbag one way and then another in Sherlock's grip. Finally, the boy steps away from him.

"I think I am fine, sir," he says quietly.

"Well," says Bell. "Well." For an instant it seems as though he is going to hug the boy for he can see by the flushed young face that fear is growing in him by the second.

"You don't need to go, Master Holmes, certainly not."

"Yes I do, sir, if I may say so."

Bell wags a finger at him.

"You shall only observe from a distance."

"Yes sir."

"Any sign of danger, any sign that you are being followed and you are to immediately retreat."

Sherlock turns to go, but Bell stops him.

"I have two more items for you. First, this."

He takes a handful of rags from the table, lifts Sherlock's hat, sets them underneath, and then replaces the fez.

"Every medical man is marked by the sight of his stethoscope bulging under his hat."

Sherlock smiles and doesn't bother to object to this little, likely undetectable detail. But Bell's other addition surprises him. He produces what looks like a horsewhip.

"This, my young friend, is a hunting crop. I was once told by a man who knew of what he spoke, that it is among the finest weapons that anyone can bear in self-defense. Hide it under your coat. If required, use it. It shall back any man away from you in an instant! Observe the wrist action."

Bell snaps the stiff, three-foot long piece of leather into the air producing a frightening crack, then turns madly on another skeleton and wades into him – his first slash knocks the skull clean from its body and sends it smashing to the floor – three boney men down in one day. Bells smiles and hands the hard black weapon to Sherlock.

The boy imitates his teacher and slices the air with another magnificent cracking sound. He seems a natural. The apothecary nods.

But immediately there is a knock at the door. The two men look at each other and Bell motions for Sherlock to hide in the lab.

The boy peers around the entrance and watches the old man open the door carefully, assuming his wide stance, with hands raised near his chest, ready to strike.

But the man who comes through the door isn't one he wants to attack.

Lord Redhorns blusters in.

"Did you receive the message which I gave your page?"

"Message?" asks Bell weakly.

"More than two days past, I informed him that you had four days in which to pay your rent or you would be summarily thrown into the streets. Do you have the funds now?"

"No, sir." Bell looks warily back toward the lab.

"I shall be here tomorrow evening. If you do not hand me the sum the instant I arrive, I shall evict you then! Good evening, Mr. Bell."

"Good evening, sir."

The door closes and the apothecary stands still. When Sherlock comes out to him, he turns with a resplendent smile. "Did you hear that, my boy?"

"Yes, sir."

"That man should go upon the stage! He is an actor whose impersonations are as marvelous as the great Macready! And a lunatic! He strolls about these parts, pretending to be a wealthy landlord! I have no idea who he really is!" Bell utters a crack of laughter.

"I know who he is, sir."

"You do?" For the first time that Sherlock can remember, the old man allows sadness to show on his face.

"And I have a plan to save us from him."

"Oh, something will turn up. I am a devotee of the science of alchemy, and of the sociological precepts of one Samuel Smiles. If one devotes oneself to bettering oneself, then life around one will always get better. And I am working on it as we speak!"

"There is a five hundred pound reward for the capture of the Brixton Gang."

Bell is speechless.

"And I am going to get it."

"I . . . I cannot allow this."

"I shall do it without nearing them. I have a way. I shall not put myself in danger."

"Do you promise, my boy?" There are tears in the old man's eyes. "You will recall . . . a promise involves one's honor. To break it is disgraceful."

"I promise," says Sherlock Holmes, "on my mother's grave."

The old man smiles and opens the front door, crouching behind so no one from the outside can see him.

"May the gods be with you, Master Holmes. Be careful and come back safely. We shall write up the evidence together, and take it to the police."

Sherlock lied to Sigerson Bell. He is going to Rotherhithe to walk straight into the lair of the Brixton Gang.

From this moment forward there will be no looking back, regardless of the danger. You either fight evil or you don't; you either get what you are after or lose it; there is nothing in between. He takes a deep breath and slips into the night.

THE ROTHERHITHE DEN

Sherlock Holmes takes a very long route to his destination. First, he heads straight north, then west, in the opposite direction he intends eventually to go, leading whoever might be following him on a wild-goose chase all the way up to Regent's Park. In the dim lights and shadows of the elm trees in that huge green leisure area he sees packs of London's poor: raggedly dressed, huddled together in groups for the night, their children wailing.

"A farthing, old sir, or just an 'alf?" begs one aged woman who approaches him on her knees, just wisps of dirty hair on her head, her face, burnt by the summer's broiling sun, the color and texture of an old leather rugby ball.

He keeps moving, hearing the faint sounds of the caged animals crying in the park's Zoological Gardens, rushes past the circles of exotic flowers planted by the Royal Botanical Society, and then plunges south, through Hyde Park, into wealthy Kensington and Chelsea, and all the way down to the river. There he passes by the lewd amusement grounds of The Cremorne Gardens where El Niño Farini first made his name in London, high in the night air. He can hear the

Gardens even though he is a quarter-mile away: the swirling dance music on its outdoor stages, the dramatic sounds of a circus at its amphitheater, and the roiling crowds.

He looks up and sees a balloon, lit with gaslights, rising above the Gardens, just as roman candles explode all around it, lighting up the banks of the river for miles. The first bang makes Sherlock jump. Oh to be there!

But instead he crosses over Battersea Bridge and begins a long journey along the south bank of the Thames, back to the frightening desolation of Rotherhithe.

It doesn't seem like anyone has been following him. In fact, he hasn't sensed a trailer since he left the apothecary's. Bell's clothes are feeling heavy as he plods along on his gigantic detour. Certain that they aren't needed anymore, and remembering that the old man had told him they were rags anyway, he slips under the bridge and frees himself of the overcoat, fez, and medical bag, tossing them into a large dustbin near the water. He starts off again, feeling lighter.

Despite lightening his load, he's exhausted by the time he reaches the southern entrance of the Thames Tunnel. That isn't good – he needs to be strong and alert. His face still aches from Grimsby's blows. He struggles along Rotherhithe Street in the dark, his eyes searching for the Asphalte Works.

He spots them, smelling worse tonight, it seems, looking darker, their black chimneys blacker. And there are the crumbling warehouses.

He crouches against the broken-down wall of an abandoned soap factory and looks across wide Rotherhithe and down the much smaller, cobblestone street that runs away from it toward the river and past the warehouses. His first plan is to try to do as much of this as he can from a distance. If he is lucky, he'll see Dante again, maybe talking to members of the Brixton Gang, hopefully doing something that gives away their identity.

But the luck that Sigerson Bell wished for him isn't with him tonight.

He waits, and no one comes. The warehouses stay black and silent except for a dim light and distant, muffled sounds in the upstairs floor of the last one near the river.

He realizes how ridiculous it is to think that he can do anything from this far away, but how unprepared he is to do much more. He has no idea what even one member of the gang looks like and the belief that they would somehow do something that would give them away doesn't make sense.

No, he has to go over there . . . right to the warehouses. There are times, his father used to say, even in the world of science, when you must gamble, when plans are not possible and nothing is certain. That's when the word *experiment* really means what it says.

Sherlock has to experiment; and hope this doesn't blow up in his face.

He rises and darts across Rotherhithe Street and onto the lane that fronts the desolate buildings. The sounds of his footsteps echo, and just like the night before, it seems there are many of them . . . more than his own. What a time, after all his precautions, to discover that he's indeed being followed! But when he looks around, no one is in sight, ahead or behind. He keeps moving, close to the buildings, all his senses alert.

Just as he suspected, there doesn't appear to be anyone inside . . . except in that last one, where those faint sounds seem to be coming from. That building is so far from the main road, and close to the river, that raised voices in its inner sanctums can't be clearly made out by passersby, unless they are right up close.

Though it terrifies him to even contemplate, Sherlock realizes that he is going to have to enter the building. All the doors on the other warehouses are broken, and knocked in, but when he gets to this last one, he can see that its entrance is closed tightly. He slowly approaches it . . . very slowly . . . then stands with his back plastered against the dirty brick wall. No one inside can see him there, even if they look through the door's little barred window or straight down from an upper floor. The sounds are indeed coming from this warehouse, somewhere upstairs. He gently nudges the thick wooden door with one hand.

It creaks open.

It must have been unlatched. That seems strange, in fact it doesn't make sense, but he crouches down and slips inside anyway. Instantly, two small figures fly at him! They are black and oily, and scream. *Crows.* They swoop past his head and out into the night, crying out as if warning him. The muffled sounds from upstairs pause for a second . . . and then resume. Sherlock lies on the dirt floor, his heart pounding. Crows always have reasons for being places; they can sense impending death and how to profit from it.

They understand evil, accept it as a part of life, especially when it is perpetrated by human beings, which is often. The crows know something is afoot in this broken-down place: the bloody Brixton Gang would be a perfect group of human beings for these clever birds to keep their eyes on.

Though it is dim in here, Sherlock can make out the room's cluttered innards: monster coils of ropes for boats, long wood poles that look like pieces of masts, moldy sections of sails, and oily remnants of steam engines. It smells earthy, and like the river.

The upstairs sounds are getting clearer. It is plain that they aren't solely human. The boy hears a dog snarling and the squeals and painful cries of other, smaller animals; and desperate scurrying and scrambling across the floor. Men seem to be encouraging them. It sounds like fighting and it frightens Sherlock to his Wellington shoes.

Perhaps it is time to go?

But he doesn't know anything of value yet. He has to get closer. He spots a crumbling staircase that rises straight up in the center of this fishy, foul-smelling ground floor.

What if I go up there?

He wants to move toward it, but can't. He is simply too scared. His whole body is shaking.

Then the big, outside door closes behind him.

Sherlock drops flat on the floor and lies as still as possible. The garbled sounds from above pause again and then resume. On the ground level, there is silence. No footsteps, nothing. Sherlock waits. Was it just the wind? But the humid night had been still outside. He twists his head around and peers in the direction of the door.

Nothing.

Going back to that entrance seems as perilous now as moving to the staircase and up its rotting steps. So he waits a little longer and then crawls to the center of the room. At the stairs, his hawk-like nose almost resting on the stinking bottom plank, he casts his eyes upward. Sweat drips off his forehead and into his eyes, making them sting. There's a board pulled across the opening at the top and a small crack of light emitting from the next floor. He can hear those horrific sounds better here; can clearly make out the dog's growls and cries of pain, the other animals' screams and whistles, and men shouting encouragement.

"Go to 'em, Killer! Face 'em, me boy! Face 'em!"

Sherlock slides onto the first step and begins to move upward, still on his belly, using his feet to secure footing on each step and push himself forward. Without warning the third step gives way and his foot goes right through with a loud crack. To him, it sounds like an air gun going off.

He freezes. The men upstairs stop talking momentarily, but then start again. Sherlock looks down at the ground floor. As he does, for an instant he thinks he sees a tall boy standing against the far wall in a top hat and long black tailcoat. Sucking in his breath, he closes his eyes hard and opens them again. The image is gone. All he sees is a greasy rope hanging on a big curving hook on that wall, just below a little shelf with a section of a black stove pipe resting on it.

He looks up again, takes another step, and feels his hair touch the floorboard. Placing his fingers ever so slowly into the crack, he tries to shove the board back, but it won't budge. *Maybe it is nailed.* He braces his feet on the step below – it feels steady – and shoves harder on the board. It loosens and snaps back, slamming down as it lands. Again Sherlock holds his breath; again the men momentarily stop talking . . . and then go on.

The boy waits for a count of one hundred before he lifts his head, very slowly, hair's breadth by hair's breadth, just high enough so he can see into the room, readying himself to leap down and run from the building. But from where he is, he can't spot anyone. He turns his head in every direction and surveys the space. There are fewer dirty remnants of the seafaring life here; in fact the floor is almost empty, its only real inhabitant, a thick layer of dust.

Moments later Sherlock Holmes is standing in the room, aware that whatever is going on up above is *directly* over him. No more than a few steps away from the opening in the floor through which he has just ascended, an old wooden ladder is propped straight up into the ceiling. Sherlock glides silently over to it. The sounds from above grow louder as he nears. He peers up. The ladder was obviously placed here after a staircase collapsed because it leads to another, sealed-off opening. This building has evidently not been in use for a long time. The trapdoor has an iron handle, and is cut just right, so the butts at the top of the ladder fit tightly into two holes.

That's where he must go.

Only now he really wonders if he should. Again, he has no idea what the Brixton Gang look like (though it sounds like four men on the upper floor, the group's exact number). What would he accomplish by actually seeing them?

But he can't report to Scotland Yard that he's simply found four strange men doing something suspicious in a Rotherhithe warehouse. They could be anyone having illicit fun – sporting men, tradesmen, even politicians or police employees. No. . . . He has to go up there and try to spot something that identifies them.

Sherlock places one boot gingerly on the bottom rung, then the next, and then the next, until his eyes are right at the handle.

Dare he lift the trapdoor?

The sounds of the dog and other animals are pitiful now – it is obvious that the canine is fighting the others. Every last beast sounds desperate.

"Lay 'em bets down, Charon!" cries one horrible voice.

Charon. That's one name.

"But the poor brute ain't got naught left in 'im! Look, 'e's puffin' like a steer! 'e's bleedin' all over the bleedin' place!"

There is laughter.

"You got enough left from the Palace job, Sutton! Lay it down!" demands a whiny, higher-pitched player.

The Palace job. And another name.

"'ow many rats left?" growls the first, rough voice.

A sinking feeling passes through Sherlock. He knows what these fiends are doing. They are pitting rats, likely dozens of them, maybe hundreds, against a bull terrier in a fight to the death; and betting on it. He's read of this sort of thing, but never really believed it happened, or if it did, that he would ever be near it. He has entered a den of evil indeed, a sort of Hades. He wishes he had the strength and the numbers to burst into that room and arrest them all.

But he isn't gaining enough evidence to do anything, not standing here blind below these fiends. He has two names, some talk of a "job," and an illegal animal fight. That might be enough to bring the police . . . or it might not. To be sure, he needs more. He has to get a look at their faces, at least one of them. He has to be able to recognize them. *No one has ever seen a member of the Brixton Gang.* Despite the danger, this is too much for Sherlock Holmes to resist. He imagines handing the money to Redhorns, the look on Lestrade's face, and the glory it will bring him.

He grips the handle with one hand and the other sneaks into his coat and pulls out the three-foot long hunting crop. It is a hard, formidable weapon, meant to get the attention of a two-thousand-pound animal. If he can use it right, bring this horsewhip violently to bear on any villain who might come at him, it may buy him enough time to get away.

He is betting that the men are enthralled with what they are doing and that he can lift up the trapdoor a few inches and look into the room undetected, only his eyes in view. He will be well ahead of any potential pursuers. When he broke into four mansions in search of the Whitechapel murderer two months ago, Malefactor had given him sound advice – to locate an avenue of escape ahead of time. He knows exactly how to get out of this warehouse: down the ladder, down the stairs, and through the maze of narrow streets. He purposely left the floor-board pulled back.

He's ready.

He pushes the trapdoor up slowly, inch by inch. He can't see anything clearly: just boots and trouser cuffs and the short wooden walls of an enclosure, obviously the pit for the animals, all lit by the soft glow of candles and a few gas lamps. The sounds almost turn his stomach. The fight has obviously been going on for a long time and the poor beasts are suffering. Sherlock hears their pitiful cries of pain and sees blood splattered on the tops of the walls. It makes him angry. He recklessly lifts the trapdoor farther up, nearly a foot.

Three men turn to him and smile. They look calm. *Why is that?* They seem to be expecting him. *Why* is that?

And where is the fourth man?

The answer comes instantly.

A big black boot, worn by someone standing directly behind the trapdoor, wedges under its elevated surface and snaps the whole thing back with a crash, leaving it wide open. An evil, whiskered face with black eyes stares down at him, smiling too.

Sherlock has seen all four members of the Brixton Gang! He doesn't hesitate. Gripping his hunting crop, he jerks his feet off the rung and slides down the ladder to the floor. He lands with a thud. But when he turns he gets the shock of his life.

The dark-dressed boy is standing directly in front of him, inches from his face, his breath as foul as a skunk's.

Sherlock thinks of the apothecary's movements when he practices his martial arts. It seems to be all about balance and leverage and getting the right distance, the distance you need to employ the weapon you have. He steps back and raises his horsewhip. He intends to lay it across this fiend's face.

But the other boy isn't interested in fancy maneuvers. He is a street person, a hardened criminal who has learned from experience how to react instantly in desperate situations. He knows to stay in close to his opponent.

"What 'ave we 'ere?"

He steps forward as Sherlock steps back, seizing the hand with the hunting crop and twisting it violently, almost snapping the bone.

"Ahhh!"

Sherlock shrieks in pain and drops his weapon. In the blink of an eye, he feels a deep sting across one of his thighs and then another, making him buckle and drop to the floor. He raises his arms to protect his face and looks up at his enemy. The other boy has the hunting crop in his hand and has stepped back; four grimy, blood-splattered men are standing beside him, forming a semi-circle around Sherlock Holmes.

"We've been expecting you," growls one of them with a horrible grin.

All that is going through Sherlock's mind is: *The Brixton Gang kills people, without thinking twice.*

18

IN WITH THE RATS

But they don't kill him, at least not yet. He knows, however, that his time is nearly up. Why hadn't he accepted Bell's offer of learning fighting techniques? While it may not have enabled him to capture these villains, he might have at least gotten away. If he comes out of this alive, he must ask the old man to teach him. But that seems beside the point – he doubts he will ever see his dear friend again.

The dark-dressed boy's appearance is clear now. He's a lad not much older than Sherlock, similar to him in many ways – black-haired, an attempt at respectability in his frayed black coat and hounds-tooth waistcoat. But he isn't as well turned out as Sherlock. His hair is unkempt, his teeth are dark yellow, almost brown, and there is a vacant, violent look in his eyes. The other four men have the appearance of modern-day pirates. Two have knives tucked into belt buckles, another has a patch over an eye, and he sees glints of gold in their mouths. All keep their hair unusually long, wear loose flannel shirts that were once white, unbuttoned well down their chests, trousers of bright colors, and sport flat straw hats on their heads. And yet, somehow they are ordinary too, much like any other desperate folk you might see on the street, with appearances that can melt into a crowd.

The two younger gang members, mere youths beside their accomplices, seize Sherlock and roughly haul him up the ladder. On the top floor they pick him up and pitch him head-first into the bloody rat pit. He nearly lands on his face, just getting his hands up in time. He is terrified almost beyond control. He wonders if he will soil his pants. He wants to cry. He wants to throw up. He needs his mother, his father, Sigerson Bell, even Inspector Lestrade. Why hadn't he at least told the apothecary exactly where he was going? Because . . . he wasn't supposed to draw close. The old man didn't expect him to be in this sort of fatal danger. His recklessness, his *chutzpah* (as the his father calls it) has put him in this situation, like a condemned Fagin in Newgate Prison waiting for the jailers to take him out to the scaffold to be hanged by his neck.

"You shall be disposed of," says one of the two older thieves, better spoken than the others, perhaps the brains behind the gang.

Sherlock wonders how they will do it.

"But we have a few inquiries to make of you first," says the other adult. He speaks well too. It is obvious that these two run things. The others – two strong lads – are the thugs.

"We have been aware of you since last night and have had your movements observed," says the first gang member with a glance at the dark-dressed boy. "We must discover what else you know."

"Before we carve you up and feed you to the fishies!" barks one of the thugs.

Sherlock wants to know just one thing before that happens. *Was it Malefactor who betrayed him?* But he can't bring himself to ask. He doesn't want to say anything that might make them hurt him even sooner than they plan.

"Crowley, Sticks, go downstairs with Brim."

The two young ones descend the ladder with the dark-dressed boy on command – discipline seems to be a strength of this group – leaving the two older men to examine Sherlock. They can see that he is trembling and it makes them smile.

"We shall be discussing matters downstairs and then we shall arise and discuss similar matters with you. Killer will watch you. This room is sealed from the inside. Don't try anything. Should you attempt an escape, we shall discover it and commence with your fate instantly."

The first one turns to go.

"Make yourself at home," says the other.

They both descend and the room is quiet. Sherlock hears them talking down below. His mind reels. What is in store for him? Will they cut off parts of his body, kill him slowly, and make him tell everything he knows as they bring him painfully to his death . . . over many hours . . . or days? He wanted to fight evil. Well, evil is here, in this building, and it isn't what he imagined – it's far worse – and it has him at its mercy.

There is blood all over the pit. The smell is horrific: animal sweat and fear and urine. At least a hundred dead rats lie in gruesome poses, some still quivering. A white bull terrier, covered with blotches of scarlet blood and terrible wounds, shivers on its haunches at the other end, eyeing him, trying to get to its feet, but falling back. *Rats are smarter than dogs.* He remembers his father telling him that. They are like the crows, hated by others for the way they look, but brilliant in their own way. Perhaps it is fitting that Sherlock should die amongst them. He begins smoothing out his clothing and combing his hair with his fingers.

Then he hears a sound up above.

There is a row of windows in the roof of the building on this floor, probably placed there to provide ventilation for what once was a very close, smelly working area. Bad air causes diseases; good air heals.

The sound doesn't seem like anything to pay attention to at first. It is barely audible, like a leaf brushing against the glass surface. When Sherlock looks up he can't even tell which window it is coming from – they are all grimy and opaque, brown like the surface of the Thames.

But then something miraculous happens. Like a moment from one of his dreams. . . . A window opens.

Someone, or some *thing*, has lifted it from the outside and propped it ajar. These windows were likely designed to be pushed wide with long poles from down on the floor, here inside.

Then a figure steps through.

It grips the frame and lets its legs hang down. Then it swings and flies just under the ceiling like a bird! Catching a beam, it swings again and flies to another, until it reaches the wall. There, it descends down the crisscrossing iron supports bars like a spider. Finally it lands on the floor, alighting without a sound.

Sherlock stares at the figure. Slowly it emerges out of the shadows at the far end and comes into the light.

The Swallow!

One of his hands is to his lips, cautioning Sherlock to remain absolutely silent, and the other is motioning for him to advance quietly toward him. The bull terrier is too wounded to make a sound. In seconds, the two boys are scaling the wall, the taller one clinging to the acrobat's back. The building has thick support beams that are suspended across the building about six feet from the peak of the roof. The Swallow mounts one and makes his way along it like Blondin with a passenger on his back. Sherlock closes his eyes. Slowly, they near the window. It isn't far away from the beam, but the acrobat will have to lean to reach it. He reaches out . . . and grips the window's frame, keeping his feet on his "high wire."

"Hold on," he whispers.

The Swallow steps off the beam.

For an instant, they hang over the rat pit far below, the trapeze star's legs swinging in the air. Sherlock's pulse races and he closes his eyes again, clinging tightly. He understands that his job is to simply hold on. Any sudden movement from him, a jerk or an adjustment, will send them to the floor. He must depend on The Swallow's expertise . . . and it is monumental.

The acrobat proceeds to perform a feat of strength that any strongman on any stage in London would be proud of – he lifts both his own body weight and Sherlock's slowly up to the open window, chinning himself. But from there, he must somehow get the two of them through to the outside.

"Hang on, I have to let go for a second," he says quietly.

What? thinks Sherlock. But he must trust the other boy. He remains perfectly still.

The Swallow releases one hand for an instant. They begin plummeting. He thrusts the same arm up and gets his elbow through the opening and onto the roof. But he can't hold on to the tiles.

They start sliding back!

The Swallow then makes a desperate move. He releases the other hand and reaches up with that elbow too. For an instant their heads are through the opening and Sherlock can smell the river in the outside air. He grabs at the tiles and gets a grip, lessening The Swallow's load.

Together they lift themselves through the opening and onto the roof.

The Swallow puts a finger to his lips again. He closes the window gently and motions for Sherlock to follow him and move the way he does. So off they go on the steep roof, on their hands and knees, heading for the river-side of the building. There, The Swallow indicates a wooden drainage pipe and within minutes both boys are on the ground, running along Rotherhithe Street, back toward central London.

Nothing is said before they reach the Thames Tunnel. The Swallow is running so hard that Sherlock can barely keep up. At the tunnel, the acrobat jimmies the lock, just like the Brixton Gang's boy had done the night before, and they enter the rotunda and descend the stairs into the underground.

"How did you know I was there? Why did you help me?"

Their footsteps are echoing downward.

"Ain't you the one who says folks should deal with one question at a time?" says The Swallow, his smile barely evident as they walk into the gloom at the southern end of the corridor, heading toward the pitch black of the center.

"How did you know?" repeats Sherlock.

"I've been following you."

Now Holmes knows why he sensed someone trailing him last night, and near the warehouses this evening.

"You're a right square bloke, Master 'olmes," continues The Swallow, his voice echoing along the cylindrical passageway, "treated me right. I intend to be on the square myself, forever. I was worried about you. I knew you wouldn't stop at just knowing 'ow the crime 'appened. I knew you'd go after . . . I knew you were a lunatic!"

They both laugh.

"I 'ad information about where the Brixton Gang was 'oled up, but I wouldn't tell anyone on me own, of course . . . thieves' honor . . . and saving me own neck!"

They laugh again.

"I didn't see you until I was near the warehouses tonight," remarks Sherlock.

"That's because I weren't following you until then. The night before I picked you up near your guvna's 'ome, got to worrying when I saw who you was following, and really worried when 'e handed you off to that snake who helps 'em. Tonight, I just lay in wait in Rotherhithe, and sure enough, you comes along. I got up on the roof and watched. When they brought you in, I made me move. I won't betray me old mates but I won't let 'em kill a young man such as yourself, either."

They are in pitch dark now.

"Yes you will," proclaims Sherlock.

His words sound up and down the tunnel. The Swallow has stopped walking. The two boys can't see each other.

"I beg your pardon, Master 'olmes?"

"You *will* betray them."

There is silence for a moment.

"No, sir, I won't."

"I need your help, Johnny. I need you to stand up and be as brave as you are on the flying trapeze."

"I am brave, sir, but I'm not stupid. In the amusement industry, we don't do what we do to die. We do it to thrill others and, most importantly, to make a living. It isn't about doing dangerous things, it's about doing safe things that *look* dangerous."

"You shall help me capture that gang!" insists Sherlock, his voice rising and resounding in the passage, "If you don't, they will kill more people, innocent people, and keep robbing others."

Sherlock needs that reward. And he'll do *anything* to get it.

"We're all thieves, Master 'olmes, in a manner of speaking. We're all evil: unfair to each other, mean-spirited. I'm sure you is no angel. In fact, I *know* you ain't."

It is a comment that angers Sherlock Holmes, perhaps because it is correct.

"That is an excuse!" he snaps. "That's what crooks and murderers say to justify what they do. I won't accept it! And I won't accept you not helping me. Come with me!"

"Where?"

"To Scotland Yard."

They start walking again, their boots trudging on the hard corridor floor, not saying anything. Soon they emerge into the lighter area and the end of the tunnel appears ahead.

"I ain't goin' with you, Master 'olmes," says The Swallow clearly. "And you can't make me. I can get away from you and you know it."

And with that he is off like a dart fired through the passageway. Sherlock is after him instantly. He *must* catch him! He can't be sure that the police will believe his story on his own – with this famous young star by his side, with the respect he commands, it would be a cinch.

But it is breathtaking how quickly The Swallow gets away. His long strides on the staircases seem to take him upward a-half-dozen paces at a time. By the time Sherlock gets up into the rotunda on the north side, the other boy has disappeared into the dark city.

Sherlock feels like falling down on the muddy foot pavement and crying. The Brixton Gang is sitting there in that Rotherhithe warehouse, ready at any second to ascend to the upper floor, find that he is gone, and flee. And what can he do about it? The clock is ticking.

In times of desperation, he sometimes thinks of his mother. "You have much to do in life" he remembers her saying, her last words before she died. They are seared into his mind.

He straightens his clothing and fixes his hair.

What can I do about it? A great deal, he upbraids himself. *I can enter the Scotland Yard offices and tell them what I know in detail. I can* demand *that they bring a newspaper writer to the scene to verify everything . . . and if they won't believe me, I . . .*

That is a tougher one to solve. What could he do if they just won't believe him? He imagines the scene at the police station – Lestrade laughing at him, throwing him in the street, allowing the gang to escape. What would he do if things went that way?

"I . . ." he says out loud, scrambling for an idea, "I . . . could steal a weapon. . . . They will have revolvers there, many of them, likely loaded. I just need to locate one. Lestrade wouldn't expect me to pick one up . . . but I will point it at his head if I must. To him, I'll be a wild boy, about to do something desperate."

Sherlock sees a hansom cab moving past, its single horse trotting slowly in the gloom, hooves clapping on the cobblestones, the driver up above the cab at the back, reins in one hand, his whip still and upright in its leather holster as he lazily watches the night.

Sherlock has never been in such a carriage. It wasn't a mode of transportation his parents could afford. But tonight he must move across London at a terrific pace. Time is of the essence. He has those two shillings in his pocket – the ones poor Mr. Bell gave him. The old man had handed them to him with a smile on his face, as if he were giving him gold. Sherlock had imagined the many things they could buy him – perhaps some new, second-hand shoes and many copies of *The Illustrated Police News*.

But he knows where the money is going now – into the coffer of that cabman. Holmes shall make him fly from where they are here, in Wapping by the river, across central London, to police headquarters in Whitehall near Trafalgar Square. His shillings should be more than enough to get him there. The streets are nearly empty – there will be a veritable racetrack stretched out before them.

Moments later Sherlock is bouncing up and down on the red, plush-covered bench inside the cab, anxiously looking out, as they gallop toward the police station.

He will do whatever he must to end the evil of the vicious Brixton Gang and save Sigerson Bell. He will take whatever chances he must and threaten whatever violence is necessary.

"To Scotland Yard!" he shouts at the cabbie. "Get there in less than ten minutes, and you keep both shillings!"

He will capture those devils. *Tonight!*

19

THE SCIENCE OF DESPERATION

The cabbie applies his whip to the horse and urges it on through the dimly lit London streets, its hooves smacking against the hard stone surfaces, foam forming on its sleek black hide, the hansom almost shaking apart. The driver takes pride in his job, but more importantly, wants to keep the two shillings he has tucked into the purse sewn into his trousers.

Inside, Sherlock watches the night go by, almost hanging out the window, nervous and anxious. He hears the sounds of violins racing, his mother's beloved instruments. They play in his head, swirling faster and faster. What is going on back in Rotherhithe? Is his prey long gone? And what will he *really* do at Scotland Yard? Will they even let him in?

He is betting that Lestrade will still be there. Malefactor knows the habits of every last detective in the London Metropolitan Police and often says Lestrade has a reputation for toiling late into the night. "An imbecile," the young crime lord calls him, "but hard-working and as tenacious as a bulldog."

The hansom flies down the hill from St. Paul's, along

The Strand, by the Charing Cross Railway Station, and turns just past the statue at Trafalgar Square. In seconds, the proud cabman is leaning down from his seat, peering through the window, announcing their arrival.

Sherlock alights. He fixes his rumpled frock coat and brushes his straight black hair carefully into place with shaking hands. He's on Whitehall, the big avenue where all the government buildings are, including the Prime Minister's residence. The front entrance to the Police Station House is on a little street just ahead. Lestrade's office is at the back on Great Scotland Yard, so he enters a narrow canyon between two buildings that opens up onto a little cobblestone square. Sherlock Holmes has never been near police headquarters before; he has always tried to steer clear of it, but now has no choice. A mist hangs in the sweaty night.

There are branch houses to the left, and directly in front, a two-storey stone structure. DETECTIVE DIVISION, reads a sign above the entrance. Sherlock sees gas lights glowing inside. Police doors are always unlocked: he races up the stone steps and opens the tall, arched entrance.

He is in a reception room in the foyer, with thick wooden chairs set against the walls, for citizens waiting their turns. But Sherlock doesn't have time for that. He has to find Lestrade. He spies a hallway leading away from the center of the room and heads for it.

"May I help you?" It's the night sergeant, sitting behind his long wooden counter.

"I must see Inspector Lestrade!" announces the boy. He is shocked at how distraught his own voice sounds.

"Tell me what this is about," replies the sergeant coolly, "and I shall decide if we will disturb the Inspector."

"He is here, then?"

"Tell me or I shall have you removed!" barks the policeman. Two burly Bobbies appear and approach the boy.

Sherlock is thinking about making a run for it: trying to get by the two big men and then darting down the hall.

"Sherlock?"

It is young Lestrade. He has stepped from an office a few doors down the corridor to see what the disturbance is about. He actually looks pleased to spot Sherlock Holmes.

"I have news!" shouts the boy, "very important news!" He steps forward and the Peelers grab him, each seizing an arm and lifting him right off his feet.

"Father," says the junior Lestrade firmly, looking into the senior detective's room while pointing at the foyer. As Sherlock kicks the air and feels himself propelled backward, the Force's top plainclothesman emerges from his office and sees the struggle.

"It's all right," he sighs, calling out to the Peelers.

They drop him and Sherlock quickly makes his way down the hall and into Lestrade's office. It is dim and cluttered inside the cramped room: full of papers sprawled across a big wooden desk, photographs of desperate-looking men on the walls, and a large map tacked heavily with red pins. Sherlock notices one driven into the Crystal Palace site near Sydenham.

The boy starts talking breathlessly, at steam-launch speed.

"The Brixton Gang killed Mercure. They robbed the Palace. I have proof. I know where they are. We can arrest them tonight!"

"Excuse me?" inquires Lestrade.

"I want the reward."

"I haven't even invited you in here yet."

Sherlock glances around. And there it is. He is in luck.

Lestrade's revolver is sitting on his desk just above the drawer at his right hand. But before it comes to that, Holmes wants to see if he can talk the detective into action.

"I will take you right to them," he sputters, "but we *must* go now and bring the Force with us. I was in the building with the gang. They had me in their hands! I saw all their faces! I know their names!"

Again this unusual boy is presenting the old detective with a dilemma. Should he believe him? Young Holmes has in his favor that remarkable effort concerning the Whitechapel murder, and against him the embarrassing interview with the Crystal Palace guard. He is flushed with excitement and it doesn't appear contrived. Lestrade wonders if he should gamble again. What does he have to lose? The party in question, after all, is the Brixton Gang.

"We have to go *now!*" repeats the ragged boy, his face pale and eyes on fire.

"Where?" asks the younger Lestrade, whose excitement is beginning to rise too. He believes Holmes, has since the moment he met him.

"To Rotherhithe," says Sherlock.

"Where in Rotherhithe?" asks the detective.

"I . . . I can't tell you, not yet, but I'll take you there . . . and . . . and I must insist that we bring a reporter."

Lestrade laughs. This is too much.

"I don't think we will be going anywhere, young man."

"Father, don't you think . . ."

"Silence!" bellows Lestrade. "This young mongrel led us on a wild-goose chase once and it will not happen again. There isn't a shred of evidence that the Brixton Gang is involved in any of this to begin with. *Find them!?* Why, all of the Metropolitan London Police can't find hide nor hair of them! It is one of this fool's fantasies!"

Sherlock spies the revolver. He takes a step so he is standing over the desk. One long reach and he'll have it in his hand. He knows he has the courage to point it straight at Lestrade's head and that the detective will consider him desperate enough to use it.

He can't let this go any longer.

"If you two *must* waste my time and have me explain why I severely doubt this," states Lestrade with a sigh, "I shall do so . . ." he turns to Holmes, ". . . as a preamble to having you dropped on your derriere on the street." He sighs again. "There are at least two problems with your ploy this evening, beyond your being completely wrong about this case in general. They are as follows. Even if you are telling the truth, then you are, first of all, asking me to accept that you have escaped the clutches of the most slippery, bloodthirsty gang

London has seen in years. And secondly . . . that they are *still there waiting for us to pick them up long after realizing that you have run for help!!*"

Sherlock knows that this makes sense. But he is desperate. He is hoping that there is some chance that the gang is still there, or that evidence can be found in the warehouse and a hot trail pursued. But he doubts now that he can convince Lestrade.

He eyes the revolver and reaches out –

At that instant, there is a commotion in the hallway, then a voice at the door.

"They'll be there!" barks a proud figure.

"The Swallow," says young Lestrade, his face glowing.

Two constables come steaming up the hall.

"Sir, he just raced past us, as quick as a bird, sir!" sputters one of them, as he and his partner grind to a halt at The Swallow's side. The boy stands erect, chest out, hands on hips.

Lestrade waves off both policemen. "L'Hirondelle," he says in a tone of respect, approaching the famous young acrobat. "What do you have to do with this and what do you know of it?"

"I know they'll still be there, sir. Move now and you can capture the Brixton Gang. Everything that Sherlock 'olmes 'as told you is the gospel truth."

Lestrade's face colors. He appears to be growing excited. He begins to pace in the tight space.

"And how do you know that?"

"I was raised in Brixton. I lived for a time in Lambeth apprenticing for a life o' crime under the notorious Ahab Spell. . . . I know two o' the Brixton Gang . . . well."

Lestrade's mouth gapes.

"I know 'ow they do things," continues The Swallow grimly. "They put Master 'olmes on the top floor of a building they was usin' for a dog-and-rat fight. Then they dropped to a lower floor to talk. They intended to kill 'im, they did. But they wanted 'im to stew first. . . . Sadists, they is. They wanted 'im to sit there all desperate-like and weepin' for hours, just to make 'im suffer, so 'e would tell 'em what they need to know before they perished 'im. They're still there. I'd wager a bar of gold on it."

Lestrade keeps pacing.

"But they won't be forever, sir. Either you go now, or you won't ever catch 'em. Every second is a lost one. They may be climbin' them stairs right now . . . or fleein' down the streets o' Rotherhithe. This is a big chance for you, sir."

Lestrade bursts into action.

He rushes to his desk, opens a drawer, pulls out a carton of bullets and seizes his revolver, spinning its cartridge and feeding it.

It wasn't loaded! thinks Sherlock.

Lestrade stuffs the other bullets into his pocket, whirls, grabs his long brown overcoat and iron bowler hat off a hook, and sweeps into the hallway, the three boys following closely behind.

"You two stay here!" he shouts at the constables. In the foyer, he calls back over his shoulder to the desk sergeant,

"Send a note down the building to Division A that I want ten men on horseback to meet me at the Southwark end of the London Bridge in fifteen minutes! I have two men with me! I want arms for all of them! And four bull's eye lanterns! Send your note NOW!"

The desk sergeant begins writing furiously.

Sherlock is full of energy, immensely excited. "And send a reporter to meet us," he growls at the desk sergeant, "from *The Times*! NOW!"

The sergeant hesitates.

"Do it!" screams Lestrade, leading his motley crew out the big black doors.

The stables are in Great Scotland Yard square not more than fifty feet away. Lestrade bangs open the doors and demands that a dozen horses be saddled immediately. Sherlock can smell the strong stench of manure. Two stable boys dive into their work.

But The Swallow doesn't follow the others into the stable. He seizes Lestrade by the coat sleeve.

"I don't want me name mixed up with this, nor do I want the Brixton Gang on me trail," he says earnestly. "I've left that life behind. You lot do this. And don't mention me name in any report or to the press. I've done me bit."

Lestrade nods.

The Swallow releases him and turns to Sherlock.

"Thank you, Master 'olmes." He pauses. "You are a star in your own right, sir." Sherlock glows. "And you taught me many things. You taught me that I can't be just part good. I have to choose. And I have done that."

Sherlock feels guilty. Could he honestly say that about himself?

"It must be awfully nice to have your brains. Developin' your mind is an exciting and admirable thing. I'm goin' to work on me own gray matter."

The acrobat reaches out and shakes the young detective's hand, then winks at him, turns the corner, and seems to vanish.

At almost the same instant, the stable boys brings two big chestnut horses forward down the main hall that separates the stalls.

"You shall ride with my son," says Lestrade gruffly.

Sherlock Holmes has never been on a horse, the gallant beasts who are the real engines of London. He looks at their strong legs and trunks and up at their dark eyes. Their backs seem very high.

After young Lestrade mounts his steed and settles himself into the front part of the saddle, feet in the stirrups, he reaches down for the other boy's hand. Sherlock hesitates.

"Come on!" shouts the Inspector's son. He seems anxious to have Holmes with him.

Sherlock grips the arm and feels himself hoisted way up onto the horse's back behind the saddle.

"Hold on!"

The horse rears up before it charges out through the wide open wooden doors and across the cobblestones. Its hooves strike the surface like gun shots. The Inspector is out in front of them.

"Hee-ah!"

They bounce violently up and down in the saddle as the magnificent animals take them flying across London. Sherlock holds on for dear life.

They cut through a smaller artery, head past the fabulous Northumberland House Hotel, by Charing Cross Railway Station again, and head down The Strand until they reach Waterloo Bridge. They cross into grimy Southwark and gallop east through winding streets, wide and narrow, racing past the denizens of the night. Sherlock sees city life from another perspective now. Faces look up at them, some frightened, dirty, and toothless; others conniving and calculating. They all know this is the Force on the prowl.

Just south of London Bridge, they pause on a street near the lawns of airy, white-stoned St. Thomas' Hospital, where the famous Florence Nightingale is in charge. They don't have to wait for long. Within minutes they hear the other ten policemen galloping toward them from the west. Holmes spies a bookish-looking, bespectacled young man holding on to a Peeler aboard one of the horses at the rear. He is clinging to the Bobbie's waist and looking both terrified and thrilled: the reporter from *The Times*! Then they are all off again, toward Rotherhithe.

"You take the lead!" shouts Lestrade at Sherlock several blocks later.

"Head to the Thames Tunnel," says the boy into his jockey's ear, "then follow Rotherhithe Street until I tell you to stop."

It grows darker as they approach the nearly unlit industrial areas. Four bull's eye lanterns bounce up and down on the sides of the horses, like big, eerie, fireflies in the night.

When the black chimneys of the Asphalte Works appear up ahead, it is time to become much more cautious.

"Slow down to a trot," says Holmes.

As Lestrade sees them ease off, he motions to his men for silence. Soon their horses are walking and Sherlock gives a signal to dismount. He can make out the warehouses on the narrow lane that runs to the river, though they are almost invisible in the hot, misty night.

"Where?" whispers the detective.

"In the last warehouse, by the water."

The men take their horses into the yard at the abandoned soap factory across the street and tie them to tethering posts by an old wooden trough. Then everyone moves like ghosts across the roadway, crouching low, lanterns spread out among the group and held close to the ground, until they gather against the soot-stained brick wall of the first building.

Sherlock is near the front with the two Lestrades. He speaks quietly into the detective's ear.

"They were on the first floor of the last building. There is a staircase that leads up to it from the ground floor and a ladder to the one above, where they had their dog-and-rat fight. There are windows in the roof on the upper floor – that's the only avenue of escape that I know of other than the front door. There are four of them plus a lad named Brim who is dressed in dark clothing and a top hat, carrying a knife . . . and a hunting crop. The two younger gang members are named Crowley and Sticks, the older, Charon and Sutton."

Though Lestrade is impressed with the thoroughness of Sherlock's report he doesn't show it.

"If they aren't there, I shall have you prosecuted for providing the authorities with false information," he mutters. He turns to the other Bobbies and motions for six to come with him to the front door of the last building and the other four, the ones with the lanterns, to spread out around every side of it.

"Look for and attend to all means of egress!" he orders urgently, but quietly.

Sherlock can only pray that the Brixton Gang is still in there. He can see the side of Lestrade's face under his black bowler hat just ahead of him as they sneak along the wall. It has turned red, sweat has come out in big drops on his forehead and along his eyebrows, which nearly touch in a bushy row like an overgrown hedge above his big nose.

Sherlock feels a tug on his sleeve. It's the reporter. He is fumbling a small, bound book in his hand but any ink and pen he might have are still in his pockets. He is breathing loudly, gulping audibly, the lenses in his little wire-rimmed spectacles look foggy, and his voice is shaky when he speaks.

"And who are you, young sir?"

"*Ssssshh!!*" hisses Lestrade, motioning for the little man to move to the rear of the group.

Sherlock's heart leaps as they approach the last building. He can see a dim light coming through the cracks in the door. Are they about to capture the Brixton Gang? Will he actually gain credit for this? Will he get his reward?

Lestrade makes the policeman at his elbow open the entrance. He is a big, burly man with a thick mustache and mutton-chop whiskers that wind three-quarters of the way down the side of his face – the strap of his coxcomb helmet is tight across the dimple in his square chin.

All six Peelers, Lestrade, and the two boys enter without a sound into the gloomy ground floor, eying the staircase dimly evident up ahead. They can smell the building's fishy inner organs. The nervous reporter follows and . . . *whacks* his boot against the wooden lip on the threshold and falls onto his face.

The sound echoes in the building.

There is a scurrying up above. Five pairs of feet are on the move.

"Police!" shouts Lestrade. "Come out and show yourselves, you scoundrels!"

As the reporter curls up into a ball on the floor, the policemen make for the stairs on the fly. *That's curious,* thinks Sherlock, *the fiends didn't douse their lights.* But almost immediately he knows why. The sounds of breaking glass come from above and then . . . the smell of gas. It is instantly pitch black. A look of horror spreads across Lestrade's face. The criminals are breaking their gaslights and putting their candles to anything flammable!

This old warehouse is a tinderbox.

"FIRE!" Sherlock shrieks.

For a moment Lestrade doesn't know what to do. His men freeze too. Should he send them blindly upstairs into what, in minutes, will be a deathly inferno, or retreat to see if the gang can be collared on their way out . . . if they come out?

He cannot miss this chance to nab the Brixton Gang!

"Upstairs!" he cries.

"No!" shouts Sherlock. But in an instant the Peelers are all scrambling up the steps. Lestrade stands stock still beneath, apparently unable to move.

Sherlock seizes the Inspector's son and pulls him to the door.

"Out!" he shouts. "Out!"

"But . . ." begins the other boy.

Sherlock hauls him violently and drags him into the street. There, they race for the river. In half a minute they are down by the water, looking up at the roof of the old warehouse. He spots the lights of two other constables moving along in the night: half of the group that was left outdoors.

"Here!" he calls out. "Gather by the river!"

Sherlock Holmes knows that experienced criminals always have a plan of escape, just as he did when he broke into homes as he pursued the Whitechapel murderer. This ingenious group, this notorious Brixton Gang, will not only have a well-planned means of getting away, but be able to execute it in a flash.

Sherlock keeps his eyes locked on the roof. Sure enough, within minutes a window opens and a head pops out. Then another appears, then another, until there are five.

"*Ssssshhh!*" Holmes warns one of the constables, who is about to shout a warning up at the building.

The five dark figures move like vermin down the roof against the night sky. They are indeed heading toward the river. Sherlock looks in that direction and sees a boat, a powerful steam launch moored there.

"Come!" says Holmes and ushers the others to a spot directly in front of the boat. As he does, he sees two more lights coming his way.

"Block the way back to the streets!" he orders them, "and get out your revolvers!"

The two constables with him pull out their own guns. Sherlock wishes he had his hunting crop.

In moments the smell of gas and smoke is evident in the humid air and soon flames are licking the insides of the open window on the roof. The Brixton Gang obviously know how to light a fire like few others, how to gas it, how to fan it quickly. Before long the building will be engulfed in flames.

Sherlock gets the men crouched low and out of sight on a stone staircase that leads to the water where the boat is tied. They are just three steps down, so they can see the scene in front of them. Looking out, the boy spots the first member of the gang leaping from the roof onto a smaller, wood-frame building. It looks like a stable and stands almost attached to the warehouse next to the river. It shakes after each fiend lands on it. Sherlock squints to see them better. They are each carrying something in their hands. He knows that two of them have knives. What do the others have? Something worse?

"Ready your weapons," he barks to the policemen.

The Bobbies raise their loaded revolvers and Sherlock can see that their hands are shaking. The building is now raging in front of them, lighting up the London night. The little laneway and the area around are illuminated like a lurid stage in a West End theater, set for a ghastly drama.

The Brixton villains are dropping down from the stable onto the ground, one after the other. Then there's the sound of their boots striking the cobblestones as they scurry across the lane for the river staircase, their heads up and alert, glancing back at the building, but ready for any trap ahead. They look calm and capable.

Sherlock can now see that four have knives and the fifth . . . a revolver.

Where are the two other lantern-bearing policemen? And what has become of Lestrade and his men inside the warehouse? Holmes glances at it as it begins to roar. Its beams will soon fall and the whole structure will collapse. *Where's Lestrade*! If the flames ignite the other buildings, a huge conflagration will rip through Rotherhithe and light up the southern shore of the Thames. Such horrific fires are not uncommon in London – and folks come from everywhere to see these shows. The crowd will be here soon: one can almost hear it rising in the night.

But Sherlock's concerns are much more immediate. The gang members don't care about what they have left behind, what destruction they have wrought . . . nor will they fret about destroying anything that lies in front of them. People like this are barely human.

The five fiends pound along the cobblestones. Sherlock peeks and sees their faces, the whites of their eyes. Down the lane he sees a pair of lanterns approaching, bobbing at the end of the other two Peelers' arms, their guns in their other hands.

But behind Sherlock an excited constable can't wait. He gets to his feet and aims his revolver. Terrified, he fires wildly and misses.

The blast of the weapon near Sherlock's ear nearly deafens him, but more importantly the officer's action gives away their position. All five criminals fix their eyes onto the figures in front of them on the stone staircase. These desperate thieves have killed people and will do it again without thinking twice. The lead gang member assesses his human obstacles in a glance as he runs, and recognizes who offers the greatest threat. As a second constable raises his gun, the criminal fires. The bullet strikes the policeman in the shoulder and he shrieks and falls. Then the crook trains his gun on the head of the first Bobbie, who immediately drops his revolver and collapses to his knees, hands thrust into the air. The villains are only yards away now and all have their weapons poised. Sherlock and young Lestrade drop too and cower on the ground, rolling out of the way to allow the Brixton Gang to pass, praying that they won't pause to use their knives or that gun.

The fiends are brutal, but not stupid. Escaping with

speed is foremost in their minds. They merely kick the two police revolvers away toward the water as they pass and race down the steps, uttering vile curses as they go.

Sherlock glances up and sees that Brim, the boy, is bringing up the rear. He is going by, with his knife out . . . the hunting crop visible, most of it jutting out of a coat pocket. Directly in front of him is Sutton, one of the two leaders.

Sherlock is terrified, but he has been disciplining himself over the past month, developing the characteristics he will need to function efficiently in the face of criminal activity. Desperate to find a way to stop this group of thieves from getting away, and to save his brilliant solution and its reward from vanishing into the night, he thinks quickly and dispassionately. The crook closest to him is a boy, whom he might be able to overpower; he thinks of the fact that the boy carries two weapons; and he remembers nasty young Grimsby's effective, come-from-behind attack. A sudden move will be unexpected – the gang members think he and the others are no longer a threat.

Sherlock rises in a flash, bends over at the waist, plants his legs, and drives forward with all the power he has, sending the hard edge of his boney shoulder into the back of Brim's knees. The boy buckles and falls face-first down the steps, smashing his teeth into the stones. As he groans and releases the knife, Sherlock enacts the next part of his plan.

Sutton is directly in front of Brim. He glances back for an instant and sees the boy with the hawk-like nose leaning over his young comrade, then reaching for an overcoat pocket and seizing the hunting crop. Almost immediately, Sutton feels the business part of that horse-whip laid across the back of his calves, not only removing a line of flesh from them and shooting searing pain up his legs, but also snaking around to the front of his knees, gripping them and, with a pull from his enemy, sending him reeling to the ground.

Sherlock Holmes is indeed a natural with Sigerson Bell's favorite weapon.

Just as he hoped, the other armed constables arrive at the staircase at that instant.

"Point your revolver at this one's head!" he shouts at the first Bobbie, indicating the wounded Sutton, now on his knees on the ground. "And seize that boy!" he cries to the other.

The gun is leveled at the leader's temple, inches away, poised to end his life. The other arriving policeman pins Brim to the ground.

But Sherlock Holmes doesn't want just these two thieves – he wants them all – every last member of the Brixton Gang. He wants to wipe them from the face of London's crime world and remove their evil blight from its midst. It's the only way to get his money.

He begins the final part of his plan.

"You three!" he cries at the top of his lungs, calling to the escaping criminals. They keep running without glancing back, racing over the muddy bank and leaping into the steam launch. But as they turn to seize the boat's ropes from the little wharf they realize that two of their lot are missing. In the light of the huge, crackling fire from the warehouse, growing in flickering reflections in the dark water, Sherlock can see the falling face of Charon, the other gang leader. That reaction is what the boy hoped for – Malefactor has told him many times that the phrase *as thick as thieves* has a great deal of truth in it. Crooks stick by one another . . . they have their code. That brutal man standing in the steam launch has a touch of good in him mixed with all his evil. He will be hard pressed to desert his accomplice, especially if it means condemning him to death.

"Lift him up!" Sherlock barks at the Peelers.

They raise Sutton to his feet, the gun still cocked and held tightly to his head.

The crowds are beginning to gather. At first there had been just a few street people, then drunks from the nearby taverns, but now many working-class folks are arriving, some in barely more than underclothes, drawn by this magnificent, deadly show. On the water, boats are drawn to the billowing flames too, as the fire adds heat to the already hot night. The sounds of the bells of the Southwark fire brigade and of their charging horses grow louder.

And suddenly, out of the nearly collapsing building, comes Lestrade and his six policemen, coughing and staggering about, one gripping a frightened and quivering reporter by the collar. The Metropolitan Police's senior detective sees Sherlock and four of his men down by the river. They appear to have two of the gang members in custody. But why is a revolver being thrust into the temple of one of them? Lestrade stumbles forward.

"If you try to escape," shouts Sherlock at the boat, his anger rising, "we shall put a bullet into the brain of your friend here!"

"No!"

It isn't the other gang leader responding. Charon simply stands stock still, his mouth wide open. It's Inspector Lestrade.

"This is highly irregular!" he cries, staggering toward Sherlock.

The boy speaks without looking at him. "Precisely! Irregularity is now in demand!"

"The Force does not condone this!"

"The Force is about to lose three-quarters of the Brixton Gang!"

The crowd lets out a roar of approval.

Standing on the boat, the evil Charon gives the order to start the steam launch's engine. A deadly contest is afoot.

Sherlock must make a decision. The boat is fewer than twenty yards away – all the players in this dramatic game of chicken can see the expressions on each others' faces – they can all estimate one another's resolution.

Charon smiles.

Sherlock hesitates . . . then decides.

"Kill him!" he screams at the Bobbie holding Sutton.

"Put the gun down!" warns Lestrade.

"Kill him!!" repeats Sherlock.

The policeman lowers his weapon.

The men on the boat are about to push off, grins on their faces.

Sherlock grabs the revolver out of the nervous Bobbie's hand and jams it into the Sutton's head again, grinding it into his temple.

"Observe!" he screams at Charon.

The leader on the steam launch turns and sees who now holds the weapon. He looks into the wild boy's face and doesn't see what he hopes for: the gray eyes are like steel, there is anger and retribution in them . . . absolute conviction . . . and a sort of greed. This lad will kill his friend right before his eyes.

"The brain is like tomato aspic!" shouts the incensed youth at the fiend. "Should I unload this piece of steel into it at the velocity my weapon can summon . . . it shall rip his precious jelly apart!"

"And I shall have you hanged for murder!" growls Lestrade.

But Sherlock doesn't even look at the senior detective, doesn't care. He thinks of his dead mother, killed by a crook, of the victim of the Whitechapel murder, of Irene nearly crippled by another fiend, of Monsieur Mercure, of all the people these devils and others like them have hurt, indeed killed. He thinks of all the evil that is perpetrated by such villains every day, ravaged upon so many decent people by the few. He thinks of his reward.

He cocks the revolver, digs it into the man's ear, and addresses the boat.

"This will be my pleasure!"

But the bang doesn't sound.

"Hold it!" shouts the gang leader on the steam launch. His shoulders sag. He turns to the others and signals for them to return to shore. Soon they are all disembarking, hands held high.

In the cobblestone lane, gathered in a huge semi-circle around the inferno and the unfolding drama near the water, a massive crowd of London's citizens bursts into applause, whistles, and foot stomping. On the water, the night explodes with fog horns and exclamations of admiration.

Sherlock Holmes looks around. For the first time in his memory, he feels a sense of pure happiness seep through him. It seems to almost reach his soul.

20

WHERE CREDIT IS ALWAYS DUE

Sherlock remains mute all the way back to Scotland Yard. It isn't because others are insisting he stay silent. Indeed, Lestrade questions him aggressively, as aggressively as he dares given the glowing admiration for this anonymous boy that was evident in the huge Rotherhithe crowd. What the senior detective really wants to do is grab the lad by the throat and throttle him, not only for his reckless, uncalled-for actions that may have made the Force look too violent in the eyes of some of the spectators, but also in order to shake the entire story of this mystifying robbery and murder out of him. Inspector Lestrade still has no idea how it transpired. All he knows is that the two crimes are apparently connected, that the entire Brixton Gang is suddenly in custody . . . that young Sherlock Holmes is about to get every ounce of the credit . . . and a five-hundred-pound reward.

"I shall withdraw the offer of money . . . if you do not come clean!"

But the boy knows that is hogwash. It isn't time to speak yet. He is holding back his story and his emotions with an enormous effort of will.

They move slowly on horseback to Scotland Yard, the reporter on a horse nearby, his presence a large factor in keeping the Inspector from thrashing the boy. Lestrade fumes as they trot onward.

At the office, Sherlock sits down to explain, making sure the journalist is poised behind Lestrade's desk with his ink bottle and pen at the ready. The detective and his son have their ears cocked, and the door tightly closed.

Holmes commences to explain, starting from the very beginning, with his observation of the doctored trapeze bar, moving on to what he learned from and about The Swallow and the other two acrobats, how he eliminated them from suspicion, how he noticed that the inside of the vault could be viewed only from Mercure's position, how he uncovered that the Brixton Gang knew The Swallow, met the guard, and then put a potion into his drink, how the whole thing was a devilishly clever crime of misdirection, secretly perpetrated by ruthless professionals while the attention of everyone in the Crystal Palace was directed elsewhere, a chaos created by their own handiwork.

He does all this without once mentioning Malefactor. Their differences are between the two of them.

Sherlock is almost done when a Bobbie knocks on the door. Lestrade motions to Holmes to keep quiet. He opens the door and the Peeler hands him a note. As he reads, a resplendent smile spreads across his face. It worries Sherlock.

When the detective lifts his eyes from the page, he is glaring at the boy.

"You," Lestrade says gruffly, pointing a finger directly at him, "leave."

"But I haven't finished the –"

"Leave!"

"With all due respect sir," argues the reporter, pulling his glasses from his face to focus on the Inspector, "he must finish his narrative."

Lestrade steps toward him, the smile back on his lips. In fact, he is trying to contain it so he won't burst into a laugh. He leans over the journalist and whispers into his ear. An expression of wonder comes over the bespectacled man's face.

"Say nothing," says Lestrade, "or I shan't take you with me."

In seconds Lestrade, the reporter, and two Bobbies are briskly leaving the police station and Sherlock Holmes is being shoved through the door. Outside, he is thrown onto the cobblestones. The London sky has begun to spit rain.

"My reward!" he cries.

The senior detective and the others climb into a police coach that has been brought up from the nearby stables, but the younger Lestrade hesitates to get in, standing near the fallen boy. He has a look of indecision on his face and moves to offer a hand and help Sherlock up.

"Son!" shouts his father, leaning out the window, looking irritated. "Are you coming with us or not?"

"But, Master Holmes helped us so much. He deserves –"

"This!" says Lestrade, pulling a banknote from his pocket and tossing it out the coach window. It lands on the fallen boy. "Are you coming with us?" the Inspector demands once more, glaring at his son. "We shan't wait."

The young man hesitates and turns back to his father. In the coach he looks out the window at Sherlock Holmes, who is still on the cobblestones, now in a sitting position, looking stunned. A dirty five-pound note lies in his lap.

What happened?

21

AWAKENING

Sherlock sleeps on the streets that night. He doesn't want to go back to Sigerson Bell until he gets the whole reward. *But when will that be?* His brain is usually able to understand or at least grapple with any problem with which it is presented, but he can't unravel this one – Lestrade's actions are a mystery.

In the morning he makes his way to Montague Street. It isn't where he wants to be. He'd rather confront the police again at Scotland Yard, or even track down *The Times* reporter.

But at this moment, he just wants comfort. His mother is gone, so affection must come from Irene Doyle. He wishes he didn't need her, wishes he was tougher, but on this morning, he simply isn't. He feels as if he were that hot-air balloon that *The Flying Man* used a few years ago to sail high above the Cremorne Gardens, only to have it suddenly deflate and drop him to the earth like a stone . . . where he died, spit upon a church steeple, of all things.

He wants to see Irene's wonderful face again, hear her strong and caring voice, and tell her that he is sorry, that he needs her friendship.

But when Sherlock turns the corner onto Montague Street, he spots three people on the far side of the road: Grimsby, Crew, and Malefactor. He hates them. He can't admit any weakness, any failure, to them, and prays they will go away.

At first, all four walk in the direction of Irene's house: the three young crooks on the east side, Sherlock on the west. He and Malefactor eye each other all the way. The young crime boss seems emboldened. He struts right up to the Doyle home and stands there – he must know that Irene is alone in the house today, as she often is, that she might come out to see him. The curtains pull back in a window on the ground floor and a face peeks out. At first, it notices only Malefactor and his henchmen and the fine white muslin material seems about to close. Then she looks out, across the street to where Sherlock is standing. Moments later, Irene descends the short front stone staircase and walks past the black wrought-iron fence to the footpath. She keeps her eye on the boy across the street.

The young mobsman near her looks pleased with himself. He takes Irene's gloved hand and kisses it. She looks ashamed and turns her eyes from Sherlock. But Malefactor keeps his gaze on him as he holds out his other hand. Grimsby produces a newspaper from an inner pocket in his coat and hands it to his boss with a grin. Malefactor is smiling too.

What is this about? wonders Sherlock.

"Master Holmes, I perceive," the young criminal genius announces across the street.

"Malefactor."

"Read the news, sir?" he enquires. "A sort of . . . hold-the-presses-early-morning-last-minute special?"

"I don't care about the news. I have a question for you that I want answered."

Malefactor yawns and puts his hand to his mouth.

"I'm sure we've heard it before."

"But you haven't answered it yet!" growls Sherlock. He strides across the street. Irene can't suppress a smile and steps away from Malefactor, moving closer to her friend. Excitement is growing on her face. Holmes notices, but tries to ignore it. He wants his answer first.

"Did you try to have me killed? Were you helping the Brixton Gang?"

"They are no longer a factor," responds Malefactor, tapping on the newspaper.

Why is he so happy about the gang's downfall?

Sherlock could understand the young crime boss being pleased, if the Brixton group was merely eliminated from the streets – there would be more treasures to go around for the likes of his mob, fewer complications, and fewer Peelers on the alert. But he must know that Sherlock played a huge role in their spectacular capture. That must disturb him deeply somewhere inside.

"You are well aware that I was at the scene of the arrest," intones Holmes, "and that it was through my deductions and actions that those fiends have been put into the custody of the Force!"

Irene glows at him.

"Oh, am I?" answers Malefactor with a smile.

Why is he acting this way?

"I asked you a question!" repeats Sherlock.

"And I told you, some time ago, that such things are mysteries . . . and shall remain so."

Then the boss turns to his two companions.

"Master Crew?" he says, handing the newspaper to his second lieutenant. "Do the honors, please."

Silent Crew, the hint of a short, toothbrush moustache beginning on his upper lip, takes the newspaper and spreads it open at the front page so Sherlock can read it. A huge black headline runs across the top.

"MERCURE AWAKES!" it shouts.

Sherlock almost staggers.

"TWO CRIMES SOLVED! BRIXTON GANG CAPTURED!" the headline continues.

"Seems the great man has roused from his brain concussion," smiles Malefactor, "and has told Inspector Lestrade what he saw in the vault room of the Crystal Palace. The good inspector then informed the press that the Force was suspicious that the Brixton Gang was involved from the start, had been on their trail for some time, and tracked them to their lair."

Sherlock is speechless. His mouth actually hangs open. He has never, in all the time he's known the Trafalgar Square Irregulars, heard the frightening Crew utter a single word. But now he does. His voice is high-pitched and nasal.

"They don't mention you," he squeaks.

"Why yes, you are correct Master Crew, they don't," adds Malefactor. "I neglected to note that. It seems that Lestrade was in possession of an extraordinary amount of information about this crime . . . and the press is more than willing to accept that Scotland Yard's hard work coupled with the submission of the only eyewitness to the crime, was what shed such a clear light upon this entire mystery and led to their brilliant solution."

"There's somethin' 'bout a boy 'elpin' out at the scene," snickers Grimsby, "but 'e 'as no name! 'em Peelers and press boys is good friends, Master 'olmes!"

There is still Irene. She looks at Sherlock with an expression of the deepest sympathy. She was with him through much of the Whitechapel case and knows what he is capable of, knows that he doesn't lie, is sure that whatever his version of the Brixton Gang's capture is, it is the truth.

The moment has come for her to reach out to him, make it all right between them. She turns away from Malefactor and steps toward him.

But Sherlock Holmes is boiling.

He cannot believe that he came here to seek comfort, cannot believe he was so weak. Comfort is not what he wants anymore. He wants his due; he wants his mother's due. He will rise from this . . . and bring down evil again in a resounding crash that no one, not Lestrade or the press or the entire populace of London will be able to ignore.

Redhorns plans to descend on Sigerson Bell today. That dirty five pounds will put him off for now. But before long, the boy will have to strike.

He violently pulls his hand away from Irene Doyle and steps back from all of them. He will work this out. He will return to the apothecary; learn Bellitsu, boxing, chemistry, build his brain every day; he will try hard at school, prepare himself to some day enter a university . . . by any means. He will outsmart them all. He will continue his plan to turn himself into a crime-fighting machine unlike any England has ever seen. When he becomes a man, he himself will be a mystery. No one will know who he really is and where he came from. He will use whatever he must to fight evil . . . even evil itself.

Irene Doyle is no shrinking violet. She has been taught independence and has a great inner strength. Her eyes harden too. She turns away from the good boy to the darker one . . . and slips her arm through his.

But Sherlock doesn't care anymore. He glares at all four of them.

"This is just the beginning," he vows. "Just the beginning."

He turns on his heels and stalks into the London day.